Socket

WINNER OF THE 24TH INTERNATIONAL
3-DAY NOVEL-WRITING CONTEST

David Zimmerman

ANVIL PRESS / VANCOUVER

Printed and bound in Canada
Cover design: Rayola Graphic Design
Author photo: Sabrina Simmons

CANADIAN CATALOGUING IN PUBLICATION DATA

Zimmerman, David

  Socket

  ISBN 1-895636-42-6

I. Title
PS3626.I54S62 2002   813'.6   C2002-910301-0

Represented in Canada by the Literary Press Group
Distributed by General Distribution Services

The publisher gratefully acknowledges the financial assistance of the B.C. Arts Council, the Canada Council for the Arts, and the Book Publishing Industry Development Program (BPIDP) for their support of our publishing program.

BRITISH
COLUMBIA
ARTS COUNCIL
Supported by the Province of British Columbia

THE CANADA COUNCIL | LE CONSEIL DES ARTS
FOR THE ARTS | DU CANADA
SINCE 1957 | DEPUIS 1957

Anvil Press
Suite 204-A 175 East Broadway,
Vancouver, B.C. V5T 1W2   CANADA
www.anvilpress.com

ACKNOWLEDGEMENTS

Because this is a first novel, I have a great many people to whom I owe thanks: Jack Gantos, whose early lessons in craft are now part of my hard wiring; Sandy Huss, for always knowing exactly which book to recommend and which line to cut; Matthew Miller, for introducing the contest to me and jumping on a plane to Venezuela at a moment's notice; Flemming Wilson, for our rambling all night talks; Diedre McNamer and Brian Salvatore, for their early belief in my potential; Paul Crichton, for all his help with my first attempts at publishing and our night time adventures in New York; Phil Deal, the most dedicated writer I know; Frances Kuffel, for firing me and making me realize I needed to get back to work; Jack and Sabrina Simmons, for photographs and dietary suggestions; Eric Nelson; David Starnes, the best officemate I ever had; Nancy Dessommes and our Friday afternoon cocktails; Ziska Burton, who suggested I go to Africa in the first place; Richard Flynn; Patty Pace, whose kindness and sharp wit helped me get back on track last year when I thought it was all over; Jeanine Hayes; Miriam; Z; Marc; the Bears; Jamie Patterson; Brett Evans, despite our present; Scott Yarbrough; whose patient editing and level headed encouragement have pulled me through many a dark spell; Charity Wilkinson; Alemu Mekonnen, a remarkable friend and the one who told me the story of trying to touch the sky to distract me from the dust while we rode on a bus through the desert; Rachel Chambers, the woman who held us together in Dilla; Telek Abebe and his hyena stones; Abebech, for her Amharic lessons and her doro wot; my next door neighbour Paul and his stories; Scott "Clifford Hayes" Simpson, the one who introduced me to Pinkie's; Joseph Thomas, the explicator of fairy tales and tireless friend; Gina and Anne-Marie (I do have a tail-it's just very small); Tina Zimmez, for her kisses, of course, and finally, my large and wonderful family, without whose support and never failing belief in my promise as a writer and a person I'd never have written a single word.

—D.Z.

For Tina and her 43 letters

1

They kill the goat with an AK-47. It comes in through a hole in the fence at the edge of the airfield to graze. At first they send a young soldier out to catch it. Planes can't land because the goat keeps flitting back and forth across the tarmac, looking for the choicest grass. I can see his mouth opening and closing, but I cannot hear him bleat. Outside the fence the hills are overgrazed and brown. Inside the fence the grass is lush and waist high in some places. The young soldier looks fourteen, but I guess he must be at least two years older. But maybe not. His uniform is much too big. It sags in the seat and knees. From where I stand, queued up beside the long glass window of the international arrival gate, it looks as though the two of them, boy and goat, are playing a game. The goat waits, grazing, until the boy is five feet away, looking up occasionally as the boy creeps closer, and then at the last possible moment, it scampers off. Sometimes they run up and down the grassy strip between the runways. This goes on for thirty minutes or more. Then an older soldier limps out onto the field. The people around me watch with interest. There is nothing else to do. We have waited for three hours to have our passports stamped and luggage inspected. We might wait three hours more. No one knows and no one seems bothered by this but me. The older soldier motions for the boy to move aside with a brusque hand gesture and slides his rifle from his shoulder. We all watch. The goat watches too, lifting its head to chew the stolen grass. The gun makes no sound, it is too far away, but little spurts of flame erupt from the barrel and the goat seems to vanish. In its place there is a red stain on the grass. Bits of fur float up and are carried away by the wind. The crowd laughs. An old man beside me claps his hands and then covers his mouth and giggles as though he has just heard a slightly off-colour joke. We go back to waiting.

2

"Please state your occupation and reason for coming to Ethiopia." The soldier scratches the stubble on his chin with my passport. Another soldier lays my two suitcases out on a wobbly card table and opens them. Two other soldiers stand behind them, elbows resting on the stocks of their machine guns. They stare at nothing. One of them chews on a pencil-sized stick with elaborate designs carved into the bark.

"I am a worker for an international aid organization. I've come to work on an irrigation project for the Addis Abeba office."

"Where is it that you come from in the United States?"

"Savannah, Georgia."

The soldier questioning me doesn't appear to have heard what I've said. He watches the other soldier poke through my belongings. His eyes are flat and dark. The colour of wet soil.

He says something to the man searching in a quiet measured voice and the second soldier pauses and looks up, uttering a single word. My interrogator smiles. The other soldier smiles. They both look at me.

"What is this?" My interrogator asks, pointing to my camera, a cheap instamatic I bought the day before I left.

"A camera," I say.

"Yes," he says. He smiles again. "This is not permitted."

"Excuse me?"

"This thing," he says, picking it up. "It is not a camera."

"Yes, it is."

"No, it is not."

"What is it then?"

"It is not permitted. I must bottle it."

"What?"

"I must bottle it."

The camera cost twenty dollars. I bought it at Wal-Mart. It is not difficult to see where this is heading. It is worth twenty dollars to me to leave.

"Yes," I say.

"It will be returned when you exit the country."

"Yes," I say. "May I go?"

"No." He smiles again. His teeth are crooked. They are the colour of eggshell. One of them seems to have grown in backwards. "You are a special case."

"I am?"

"Yes. You must go to the Donkey Room."

"The Donkey Room?"

"Yes." He says something to the soldiers behind him and they come around the table. One of them takes a hold of my elbow and the other closes my suitcases and slides them off the table. I notice that several pairs of socks are on the floor beneath the table and I open my mouth to mention this, but think better of it. As we walk off, my interrogator waves and smiles again.

"What is the Donkey Room?" I ask the soldier who is leading me by the arm. His face is perfectly round and slightly shiny with sweat. He does not answer.

3

_____

The Donkey Room is beige. It looks like a police interrogation room from a 70s cop show, only much dingier. There are smears of grime which ring the walls at shoulder height. There are two chairs and a scarred wooden table. One of the chairs is broken. The door is locked. I wait here for two hours. I sit on the good chair and read *Great Expectations*. I've never read it before and it makes me laugh despite my nervousness, which has reached a trembling state just below panic. The book was a going away gift from my sister. I chew my finger-nails. The socket behind my glass eye itches. I take the eye out and lay it on the table, but I do not scratch. I know from experience that scratching will only make it itch more. I lost the eye five years ago. The itch is imaginary. It sometimes comes when I am tired or anxious. Although the floor of the Donkey Room is filthy, I see no cigarette butts and so I don't smoke for two hours. The craving gnaws at the flesh of my lungs. Moments after I light the first cigarette the door opens.

Shit, I think. I want it to be over; however, I don't want to have the experience that will make my waiting come to an end. The two feelings are equal. They are balanced at the tip of my cigarette.

Two men come in. One is dressed in a dark sports coat and a red V-neck sweater with a small, ragged hole at the point of the V. He wears glasses with heavy, black frames. He is perhaps fifty years old, but it is impossible to tell with any certainty. He might be sixty or even thirty-five. The second man wears a uniform, but it is several shades lighter than the ones worn by the soldiers who searched my bags. The man in the civilian clothes looks back and forth between my glass eye and my empty socket. He has opened his mouth to speak, but the glass eye distracts him. It is the soldier who speaks first.

"You must now remove your clothing." He has learned English from an Englishman and his voice sounds stilted and strange. I fight the temptation to smile. I am slightly giddy from the worry and the waiting.

"Why?" I ask.

"Please," says the other man. "Do not make trouble. This is routine."

I take off my clothing slowly, folding each piece deliberately, as though this might normalize the situation. My nervousness becomes outright fear. It tastes like a penny in my mouth. I find it hard to keep my expression neutral. When I am finished, the soldier goes through the pockets of my clothes, overlooking a secret pocket sewn into the inseam of my pants filled with $500. He speaks to the man in the jacket softly, rapidly. The man responds with a sucking sound, a quick intake of breath. The room is warm, hot even, but I am cold. My leg jitters and I fold my arms across my chest.

The man in civilian clothes examines me closely, but does not meet my eye. The soldier methodically searches my bags. When he comes across the black leather bag, which holds my toiletries, he takes a narrow knife from a sheath on his belt and cuts out the lining. Plastic prescription bottles clatter onto the floor. Malaria medicine, codeine tablets, antibiotics.

"Tell me please why you are here?" The civilian straightens his tie and smoothes it under the sweater. His lack of a uniform worries me, although I don't know why. The soldier continues to inspect my belongings. By now he has looked at each object twice. I am relieved to see the cash in my money belt holds no interest for him.

I repeat what I told the other soldier.

"Yes," he says, "but to which organization?"

"ADO," I say. "The African Development Organization. It is based in Italy."

"Yes, I am familiar with this group. Why do we not have your name?"

"I don't know."

The man looks at me. There is nothing in his expression for me to read.

"There is supposed to be a car waiting for me outside. I was told that Dr. Otto Cavarri would be waiting for me at the airport."

"There is no one waiting for you."

"Perhaps he has left. I've been here for almost eight hours. I'm sure that someone at the office could verify what I've told you if you call them."

"That is impossible. An Oromo terrorist group destroyed the Central Telecommunication Building this morning."

"Well," I say, moving from foot to foot, "we could go there in person."

He stares at me for several long moments. There is a faint, white scar running from the corner of his eye up to his hairline. I am no longer frightened. I am uncomfortable and angry. I want to shout: *Listen, you dumb asshole, you've gone through my stuff. I have nothing to hide. Just let me get the fuck out of here.* Instead I chew at the inside of my cheek. He takes off his glasses and polishes them with the hem of one of my shirts.

"Put on your clothes."

I do. Much more quickly than I took them off.

He gestures toward my belongings, which are strewn across the table and the dirty floor. "Put your bags in order. We are finished."

I am repacked and ready in no more than three minutes. They open the door and walk out. I follow them, dragging my suitcases behind me, bulging like pregnant golden retrievers.

"Go," the man says, as I follow them back toward the arrival gate. "We are finished. You do not need to follow us." He snaps his fingers and points in the opposite direction.

It is dark outside. In the distance, the lights of Addis Abeba flicker. The air is chilly and smells of wood smoke and damp asphalt. I trudge across the parking lot looking for a cab.

4

The Wabe Shabelle Hotel is one of the tallest buildings in
Addis Abeba. Its name flashes in huge red letters on the top
of the building and is visible even from the outskirts of the
city. The lights that make up the S have burned out. My
room is large and commands an impressive view of the valley. It smells of mildew and damp, like an airless basement,
and there is a path worn in the orange carpet between the
bed and the bathroom. There is a television, but it doesn't
work. The channel knob looks as though it has been melted
with a blowtorch. I haven't eaten since I got off the plane.
My stomach makes noises, but the hotel kitchen has closed
and I'm too tired to venture out into the dark unknown.
The only thing that keeps me awake is the leftover edginess
from my experience in the airport. I take a shower and fall
asleep immediately.

5

I waste three hours looking for the ADO office. Most of the
streets in Addis do not have names, so the cab drivers orient
themselves using the names of neighbourhoods. Since I was
never given this information, it takes five or six fruitless cab

rides to find the office. The last cab driver speaks a little English. He smiles a lot and winks at the end of each phrase as though there's something vaguely naughty about what we're doing. There are two parallel scars, like the number eleven, cutting down through his left eyebrow. I like him. He calls money 'corn.' As in, it will cost you fifty corn for me to take you there. I'm almost certain this is too much, but since I don't know the standard rate, it's impossible for me to negotiate. We drive in widening circles through the city. Sometimes he stops the car to run inside a building and ask for directions. No one has heard of ADO. Finally, we go to the English Embassy and he asks a guard posted outside the gate. The guard thinks it is near the football stadium. It is not, but a Swedish man standing on a street corner nearby the stadium knows where it is. By the time we find the office, my skin is gritty with diesel exhaust and my head is throbbing. The sky is the colour of diluted milk, but the light still bothers my eye. It is somehow worse than direct sunlight.

The ADO office is located in a neighbourhood called Arat Kilo. It is across the street from the national university, on the second floor of a crumbling stucco building striped with orange stains in the places where the gutters leak. The door to the office is ajar, so I step in without knocking. I'm out of breath. The air in Addis is thin because of the altitude and I've just run up the stairs. The sitting room is hazy with cigarette smoke. Two Ethiopian men pore over a map spread out on the reception desk. They argue in shrill voices for several moments, sometimes violently jabbing their fingers at various parts of the map, before they notice me.

The taller of the two wears a faded blue T-shirt with the words 'Rod Stewart thinks I'm sexy' written on it. "Africare is moving to Bole," he says this without looking up.

"I'm looking for ADO."

This seems to startle him, but he doesn't respond.

"We are closing," the other one says. He has puffy, un-combed hair and three painful looking boils on his left cheek.

"I'm here to see Dr. Cavarri. He's expecting me. In fact—"

"Dr. Cavarri is going," the taller man says, glancing up briefly and then looking back at the map.

"When will he be back?"

"He is going." He slides his palms back and forth across each other rapidly as though dusting them off. "There is no more Dr. Cavarri in Ethiopia."

"I don't understand."

"He has a sickness," the other man says. "He is going to Italy and no more coming here."

"I have to speak to him before he leaves."

The taller man makes a sound of disgust. "He is leaving already. Two weeks ago."

"But I just spoke to him. It must have been—" I stop, realizing that it was almost exactly two weeks ago that I spoke to him. He sounded fine on the phone, but what does that mean? Nothing.

I have captured their interest. Both of them stare at me. Their scrutiny is more uncomfortable than their indifference.

"I'm Ronald Percy."

Neither of them says a word. Their expressions do not change.

"Do you work for ADO?" I ask.

"Of course," the taller man says, as though this were ridiculously obvious. "I am the driver."

"I've come to work on the irrigation project with Dr. Cavarri. Someone was supposed to meet me at the airport yesterday, but no one came. Is Mr. Trevello here? Maybe I can speak with him." Mr. Trevello is the assistant director.

"Ato Trevello is in Shashomene," the smaller man says.

"When will he be back?"

"Soon."

"Today?"

"Tomorrow or the next tomorrow."

I'm suddenly exhausted. There is a wooden bench beside the door. I sit down.

"You cannot sit there," the taller one says, stepping out from behind the desk. "We are closing."

I rub my good eye. Jesus. "Look, I work for ADO in the United States. I was sent here to work on a project. I was told someone would meet me at the airport. No one did. I spoke to Dr. Cavarri on the telephone two weeks ago. He said everything was arranged. He said there would be a house ready for me. Isn't there anyone I can talk to about this? Who else works in this office?"

"What is your eye?" the smaller one asks. He points. "It is looking broken."

"Never mind my eye. I need to talk to someone—" My voice has become loud and sharp. I stop. I can't start yelling. This isn't their fault. It's just a mix-up.

"Did someone kick you in the eye?" the taller one says. "My mother's brother. He has a kick in the eye and now nothing in the eye."

"The eye is glass," I say, taking it out and handing it to the taller one. "Who can I talk to? There must be someone here."

The two of them speak to each other in Amharic in excited voices and pass the eye back and forth. The smaller one rubs it against his cheek. The cheek with the boils.

"It is a very beautiful eye," the smaller one says. He rubs it over his lips. For a moment I think he's going to pop it into his mouth.

"Where is everyone?" I ask. Through a half-open door, I can see a series of ramshackle cubicles lining the walls in the office behind the reception room. Each and every one is empty. A telephone rings somewhere in the back, but neither of them moves to answer it.

"Shashomene," the taller one says. I take back the eye, but I do not put it in the socket. It makes me feel a bit guilty, but I don't know what they've touched before they touched the eye. I worry about infection. An infection in the socket would go straight to the brain. I have a sudden vision of the socket contracting an exotic fungal infection and becoming furred with orange mold. I put the eye in my pocket.

"Tomorrow," the taller one says.

"Maybe," says the other.

6

I eat fried meat with my hands in dingy cafés, twisting it up in the flat pancake-like bread called *injera*, which is served

with every meal here. *Injera* is tangy like sourdough bread
and lies heavy in the stomach. I walk the streets. Everywhere
I go I am distinctly aware of being an outsider. Women,
wrapped with white scarves that are as loosely woven as
cheesecloth, shrink away when I pass them on the sidewalk.
Old men draped in dirty white blankets cluck at me. Flocks
of homeless boys trail my every movement in the city. I have
been to Third World countries before, but never have I seen
so many homeless children. They are there when I leave the
hotel, and as I move through the city their numbers grow.
Sometimes there will be as many as twenty. There is nothing
I can do to make them go away. *Ferenji, ferenji,* they say.
Fuck you, thank you, please, money, I love you. They have
collected these words the way a crow will hoard bright bits
of cloth or tin foil. Twice they follow me into bathrooms,
only leaving when I bellow and shake my fist. They take
turns kissing my hands and rubbing the hair on my legs the
way you would pet a cat. *Chuck Norris, Titanic, fuck you.*
The only young men in this city are soldiers, and they are
on every corner. I see a man with an open wound in his
belly, which allows his large intestine to protrude pink and
glistening. He lies on a square of cardboard with an outstretched hand. He is always on the same corner. I pass him
every day. I drink coffee as thick as mud and as strong as
Benzedrine. Pickpockets steal my sunglasses. I walk through
warm mornings of blinding sunlight and cold wet nights.
Herds of goats with numbers spray-painted on their sides
are blocking traffic everywhere. On the third day a convoy
of tanks and trucks rumbles through the streets, bringing
the life of the city to a halt. Muslim calls to prayer are

amplified by scratchy public address systems and accompanied by wails of feedback. They come just before dawn and
just before dusk. I spend aimless afternoons in the company
of CNN and warm beer in the lounge of the hotel. I eat
spicy red stew. I suffer through diarrhea, cold showers, an
itchy socket, and general unfocused anxiety.

7

I go back to the office twice a day over the next week and a
half. It is always locked. No one answers the door. Once I hear
someone moving around inside and I yell out who I am, but
they do not come and let me in. The clerk at the hotel explains
that telephone services are still disrupted. The only free lines
are reserved for government officials. I cannot contact ADO's
office in the United States. I wonder if I'm even in the right
country. What other country sounds like Ethiopia? Eritrea?
Maybe the entire venture was flawed before it began by a mis-
pronounced word on a fuzzy international line. The American
Embassy claims to know nothing of the situation. They've
never even heard of my organization. The woman I speak to
advises me to sit tight or go home. Something will happen,
she says. You just have to keep in mind that this is Africa.
Misunderstandings are a part of daily life. Plus, there's a war
going on and God knows how many ethnic disputes. She rec-
ommends an Italian restaurant and several tourist spots for me
to while away the time. Give it a couple of weeks, she says. I
make an awkward play for a date and then notice her wedding

band. She laughs it off and tells me she'll call USAID, which
has an office on the other side of town. They've never heard
of ADO either. I begin to wonder if I haven't imagined the
whole thing myself. She won't let me use the embassy line to
call the United States. It is not an emergency, she says.

8

On Thursday the office is open. A young Ethiopian woman
sits at the reception desk typing on a word processor with
blue stencilled letters on the side which reads, Property of
the Canadian Government. She is as small as a ten-year-old
girl. Light skin and high cheekbones with braids the width
of electrical cords falling to the middle of her back.

"May I help you?" she says, looking up at me for a brief,
hesitant moment and then looking down at her desk. Her
voice is so soft I must lean in to hear her.

I tell her my story and she nods her head as I speak. She
is attentive and courteous and I'm ready to fall in love with
her just for that. When I am finished, she clasps her hands in
her lap and shakes her head. There is a small, blue tattoo of
a cross on the webbing between her thumb and forefinger.

"I have not been informed," she says.

"May I speak with Mr. Trevello? Is he here?"

"Ato Trevello is very busy."

"Yes, I understand, but I've come here from America to
work in this office. I've been waiting for more than a week.
Would you tell him I'm here?"

She raises her eyebrows, makes a small, soft sucking sound and then slips back into the offices, shutting the door behind her. Before it closes, I hear voices and the rattling of an electric typewriter. She is gone for nearly fifteen minutes. When she returns, she beckons with her hand and says, please.

Mr. Trevello has a nose as flat and wide as a turnip. He stands when I come into the office and embraces me with thick, muscular arms, crushing me up against his massive belly. His breath smells like beef stew and alcohol.

"Ah, yes. You are the one Girma told me about. He is very fond of your eye."

"Mr. Trevello," I say, "there seems to be some confusion. I spoke to Dr. Cavarri several weeks ago about my position here. No one seems to know anything about it. I was expecting to find—"

"Yes, yes, this is terrible. We have been having many problems. Dr. Cavarri left rather suddenly and he did not inform any of us about your arrival."

"Even still, the irrigation project has been in planning for more than a year. Someone must have heard something."

"Irrigation project?"

"The eastern irrigation project in—"

"There are so many projects. It is hard to keep track. I, myself, just came back from a tour of well capping projects."

"But this project is huge. Your government has allocated some $500,000 for it."

"Excuse me? How much?"

"Five-hundred thousand. It strikes me as peculiar you don't know anything about it."

Trevello purses his lips and squints his eyes. "Dr. Cavarri did not always inform us about the happenings in the home office. There have been some," he grimaces, "irregularities. We haven't spoken to the home office in at least six months."

"That can't be true. Mr. Amalfitano at the Rome office told me he was in constant contact with Dr. Cavarri. I called here myself three weeks ago."

"When is this money coming?"

"The money? The money is here."

"When?" His voice rises an octave.

"I don't know exactly. Two months ago? The materials were supposed to have been purchased by now. I've come to deal with logistics."

The skin around Trevello's eyes tightens. "Do you have identification?"

I dig my various I.D. cards out of my money belt and hand them to him. He takes a pair of cracked reading glasses out of his shirt pocket and arranges my cards in the shape of a triangle on the desk. "Ahh," he says, "this will take time. As you know, the telecommunication building was bombed."

"In the meantime, where do I stay? Dr. Cavarri said—"

He dismisses this with a wave of his hand. "You should just stay at a hotel. Keep your receipts."

"I'd rather find something more permanent and comfortable."

He laughs without amusement and folds his hands on his belly. His shirt is so tight his skin is visible between the buttons. "More comfortable? In Addis?"

"At least more permanent. Where do you put up visitors from the home office?"

"We've never had visitors from the home office in the three years I've been here."

I know for certain that this is a lie. The week before I left I spoke to three people who had come just the previous year. It is such an unlikely lie that I don't know how to respond.

"However," he sighs and cracks his knuckles, "Dr. Cavarri's house is now vacant. If you wish, you may stay there for the time being, but I must warn you there are no servants."

"I'll manage," I say.

"Why don't you go and settle in now? I'll have Girma drive you over to the hotel to pick up your belongings. I have a friend in the Department of Agriculture who may be able to let me use an international line for a quick call. He owes me several favours." He smiles, showing me his yellow stained tongue. It is as fat as the tongue of a boot. "There are some open, you know, they are just restricted to government offices."

"Yes," I say. Even though I am more baffled than before about the situation, the fact that I've actually spoken to someone about all this and the prospect of a permanent place to stay have cheered me up considerably.

He stands and calls out the door for Girma.

9

Girma wants to know what I do with the eye when I sleep. I tell him I soak it in a glass of water. The eye is all we talk about. He wants to touch it again, but I pretend not to understand.

We pick up my bags and drive west. First, taking paved roads ravaged by potholes, and then mud lanes barely large enough for the Land Cruiser to negotiate. A thin rain falls and the air is cool and pleasant. I roll down the window, but Girma insists I roll it back up again. He tells me that fresh air is full of disease. His mother died because of a draft. He shakes his head in disbelief over my ignorance of such basic facts.

The city sprawls out in strange ways. Brand new glass and steel office buildings are surrounded by acres of muddy slums, yet still lack a paved driveway to their entrances. Neighbourhoods of tiny shacks built in the median strip of large roads are constructed completely from refuse. The shanty towns trickle through the city and pool like clotting blood on unclaimed wasteland. The compound walls of large houses and churches are the fourth wall of many shacks. There are no streets in these shanty towns, only packed clay paths. We've been driving for forty minutes, but there seems to be no end to them. The shanty towns stretch along the valley floor for miles and miles.

We pick up another paved road, which runs past the Normal College for secondary school teachers. It is built on a steep rise at the edge of the valley. We pass boys herding piebald cattle and old women picking their way down the hillside with bundles of kindling tied to their backs. The air smells like rotten fruit and cooking fires. I am on the verge of asking Girma where we are when he points to a drab olive coloured building ahead of us. It is a large stucco structure, sagging on the side of the hill. Girma parks the car and unlocks the gate. The house is enclosed by a thick, concrete wall that is topped with shards of broken glass. We drive up to the door. Girma takes my bags and places them on the doorstep. Before I can even unlock the door, Girma is down the steps and getting into the Land Cruiser. He backs out onto the street, waves to me and locks the gate behind him. It occurs to me that I don't have a key to the gate.

10

The smell is so thick I can taste it. It sends me reeling backwards. I trip on my suitcases and tumble down the steps, raising a tendril of gray dust. For a moment I think I might vomit. I spit several times and then the feeling passes. The smell is unlike anything I've ever experienced. It is the smell of garbage juice at the bottom of a trash can in mid-July. It is the smell of a poisoned rat trapped in the wall of a house. It is the smell of a butcher shop dumpster. It is the smell of a portable toilet broth simmering on a stove. It is the smell of all these things combined and condensed. Sweet and vile and somehow distinctly human. I'm not sure I can go inside again. Even ten feet away with the door barely cracked, the smell reaches me.

11

I stop up my nose with toilet paper soaked in aftershave.
This helps, but not nearly enough. The rooms are dim and
bare. Their walls are pale, butter yellow trimmed with green.
Only the palimpsest of the previous tenant remains in the
form of thick shadows of dust on the floor where furniture
had stood for many years and was then removed quickly.
There are darker spots on the wooden floor where rugs once
laid. I pass from room to room. Each one is as vacant as the
last. In the kitchen there is a broken pair of scissors and a
cracked ceramic jug. On the steps to the second floor there
is a dog-eared copy of an Italian translation of a John
Grisham novel. The wood creaks underfoot. Somewhere outside a woman calls her child like a keening bird. The smell is
stronger on the second floor, which is simply a hallway letting onto a series of bedrooms. In one, there is an orange
tabby cat licking its back. It darts out a broken window and
scampers across the roof when I pass. All of the doors are
open except one, midway down the hall. Each door is painted a different colour. Avocado, peach, lavender. The closed
door is painted gold. I touch the doorknob. I wonder what I
would be doing at this moment if I hadn't left the States to
come here. I would be drinking heartburn coffee and filling
out forms. I open the door. I gag.

The smell is as palpable as smoke. I can almost see it

hanging in the air. I light a cigarette, hoping this will cover
the stench a little; but it does nothing. The room contains
its original furniture. A large bed made of wrought iron. A
rosewood writing table. An armoire that looks like it was
carved from dark chocolate. There is a dressing table in the
farthest corner upon which is laid out an old fashioned
men's toilet kit: a silver backed brush, a hand mirror, a razor
and strop, several cut glass bottles of cologne. The room is
small, and from where I stand in the doorway, there is no
obvious cause for the smell. There is a frenzied confusion of
flies in the air, buzzing and whining and thumping against
the windowpanes. I cover my mouth with the hand holding
the cigarette and step into the room, breathing only tobac-
co smoke. The flies are on me at once. They land on my
arms and cheeks and try to crawl into my mouth and nose.
The sensation of the flies on my face is almost as disgusting
as the smell, but I am curious about the objects on the
dressing table. The toilet kit is monogrammed with the letters O.L.C. These seem to be the former director's initials,
but the set is very old and looks expensive. It seems odd he
would leave these items behind, and even more odd that no
one has stolen them.

I'm reaching to pick up the mirror when I hear it. A very
slight, sticky sound of movement. I bend to look beneath
the bed. Underneath is a red and gray striped necktie form-
ing the shape of a G in the dust. The bed is unmade and
rumpled. A blanket is piled in a mound at its foot. I lift the
blanket and immediately vomit. My cigarette drops into the
mess I've made and goes out with a hiss. The blanket is hiding the body of a child. The skin undulates with the

movements of a thousand tiny worms. It is impossible to tell
how old the child was or to determine its sex. The face has
been bludgeoned into an unrecognizable puddle of flesh.
My disruption of the body incites a furious riot of flies.
They fill the room with the sound of a television tuned to
an unused channel.

12

The first policeman does not speak English. I talk at him for
almost five minutes before I realize this. He just smiles and
nods his head. He could not possibly be older than nine-
teen. We walk to the nearest small patrol station, a cinder
block shack with a tin roof. Two middle-aged men sit drinking coffee. One of them wears pajama pants and a khaki
uniform shirt. The other has his boots kicked up on the
desk. The man in the pajama pants is relating a story that
makes the other man burst into laughter. An elderly woman
squats beside a portable charcoal stove, fanning it and
occasionally adjusting a brown clay pot propped on the
coals. She also smiles at the story. Everything stops as soon
as I enter the room.

"Hello," I say, uncertain how to proceed now that I am
here.

"Hello," the men say.

Once again I tell the story only to discover upon finishing
that neither man speaks English. They watch me with fasci-
nation. At the conclusion of my story, there is a long

moment of silence. The old woman refills the men's cups with coffee and then pours one out for me and one for the young policeman who has brought me here. The cups are tiny and have no handles. I set it on the desk to let it cool. Another man comes in. He is tall and almost neckless because his shoulders are so broad. The men sit up straight. The woman lowers her eyes. He looks at me as though I am something distasteful he has inadvertently picked up on his shoe.

"What?" he says.

"Do you speak English?"

He holds out his thumb and forefinger and squeezes them together repeatedly to show that he can speak just enough English to pinch someone.

"I have found a dead body," I say.

He looks at me for a moment and then speaks to the room in general. The boy who led me here responds. His voice is barely audible. The chief cuts him off and speaks in an irritated tone. The boy lowers his head. I touch the chief's sleeve and point in the direction of the house. He shouts at me so loudly and suddenly that I jump back against the desk and spill my miniature cup of coffee. I decide to leave. If they take the trouble to follow me, I'll lead them to the house. If not, I'll try to find my way to the American Embassy and explain the situation to them. As I'm stepping out, I realize that this should have been my plan of action all along. I don't know what I was thinking coming to the police station.

The world seems to have tilted slightly since I've been in the police station. Everything outside feels unreal, slightly off kilter. The colour of the landscape—grass, sky, trees, walls—is washed out. The sun looks wrong, but I couldn't say exactly how. It requires effort simply to walk normally. The chief is speaking, maybe to me or maybe to the other officers, but I continue walking. When I reach the street, the feeling of relief is absolute. It clears my head and I feel much better. That was a very bad idea, I think, but now I'm safe. Then I see that the chief and the younger policeman are behind me. There is nothing else to do about it but beckon for them to follow me.

When we reach the house, I remember I had to climb the gate to get out. The policemen are walking about fifteen paces behind me. There is no way to explain this except by example. The chief shouts at me when he sees what I'm up to, but by the time he reaches the gate, I am on the other side. He shouts at the boy and he shouts at me. The boy runs off in the direction of the station. I point to the house. I walk up the steps and unlock the door with my key, hoping this will show him I do have permission to be here. He climbs the wrought iron gate, rattling the padlock as he heaves himself over the top. I wait at the foot of the stairway inside until he reaches the door and then I continue up the steps. His expression changes once he enters the house. He covers his mouth with his hand. I won't go back into the room. I point to the door. He pushes past me and enters. There is a coarse, guttural coughing sound and the chief re-emerges. His mouth is slack and his eyes are red. We stand silent and look at one another. I hold my breath. The world turns once. The seasons pass. I feel my hair losing its colour, my teeth falling out one by one. The only sound is the buzzing of flies, but it is curiously amplified, as though it is playing over the speakers of one of the public address systems used for the daily prayers. He doesn't move, but his eyes change. He has stood in judgment and found me wanting. I want to disappear, shrink into the floorboards and vanish. I fight the urge to turn and run. My stomach feels like it is filled with wet cement. What little control I had over the situation has now slipped like a sweat-slick pencil from my fingers. He grabs me by the shoulder and drags me down the stairs and out into the milky blue sunlight of an overcast February afternoon.

13

The police car is a tiny Fiat with a siren on top. There are six men inside. All but two get out. The chief is shouting again. Flecks of spit splatter my cheek. I'm taken by the collar of my shirt and shoved into the back seat. The chief pulls the man in the passenger's seat out of the car in a similar fashion and sits down. He slaps the dashboard twice and the car lurches into motion. I have not been handcuffed. That must mean something, I think. The car rocks and creaks over the potholes. A small boy herding sheep spies me in the back seat, points his herding switch at me and commences to shriek with delight. Another little boy comes out of a nearby hut and the two of them run along the side of the car shouting, *ferenji, ferenji, ferenji*. The chief struggles to turn around in his seat, takes a handful of

my hair and slaps me so hard my lip splits and my ears
buzz. Then he turns back around and mutters something to
the man driving. They laugh in the hard way of policemen
and soldiers. There's nothing to it but the sound.

14

I'm scared, but the feeling is useless and exasperating. We
drive across the city in relative silence. Sometimes the driver
lets out what sounds like a curse and lays on the horn. It is
five o'clock and the streets are clogged with cars and deliv-
ery trucks and wagons pulled by donkeys. When the traffic
bothers him too much, the driver pulls up onto the sidewalk
and drives past the congestion. Pedestrians have to leap to
avoid being hit. We turn a corner and I recognize where we
are for the first time. The Mercado. The largest open air
market in Africa. But then we turn again and go down a hill
and across a small stream, which is lime green and congealed
with sewage. I wonder if the chief is just waiting for a bribe,
or, if not, how likely the possibility is I could bribe him. I
have nearly a thousand dollars in American currency. Half of
it is tucked into a pocket sewn into the inseam of my pant
leg. The rest is in my money belt with my passport. I consider
it for a time, but I don't do anything for fear of making the
problem worse. The road follows the stream for a quarter
mile, breaks right and zigzags up a steep hill. On either side
are enormous eucalyptus trees. The houses begin to look
more rural—mud walls and thatched roofs instead of scrap

wood lean-tos topped with shingles made of flattened cans.
At the top of the hill, the road levels out. We turn off the
asphalt and drive up to an iron gate guarded by several men
with machine guns. They roll back the gate and wave us in.
Through the open window comes the sound of gunfire.
Short controlled bursts. It is impossible to tell where it's
coming from. We stop at a white wooden building with a
porch that wraps all the way around it. It has the look of a
colonial farmhouse. A tree the width of our car stretches up
over the house. Its branches are full of pale green fruit. The
driver and I stay in the car while the chief goes into the
house. He remains inside for the better part of two hours. As
soon as the chief leaves, the driver pulls a pink plastic bag
out from under the seat. Inside are what look like the trim-
mings from a hedge. He hums quietly and pulls the smallest
leaves off the twigs and stuffs them into his cheek.
Occasionally, he pours what looks like salt or sugar into his
mouth from a twisted gray cone of paper. When his cheek is
full, he hands the bag to me and nods. I don't have any idea
what it is or where it's been, but I do know that rejecting his
hospitality could be dangerous. I pluck the leaves off and fill
my cheek the way he has. They are bitter and coarse enough
to irritate my split lip. I hand the bag to him and he gives
me a bottle of Fanta orange that he has opened by knocking
a hole in the cap with a nail. It is warm and flat, but I'm
thirsty. The small hole prevents anything but the smallest
taste. I nurse it for a moment and pass it back up. He smiles
at me, then he turns around to stare out the window until
the chief comes back. As soon as I can do it without attract-
ing his attention, I slip the wad of leaves out of my mouth

and tuck them in between the seats. The bitter taste stays in my mouth, like I'd been sucking on Tylenol tablets.

The chief returns with a man in a shiny, black suit. This new man opens the door and sits down beside me in the back seat. He smells like stale sweat and Old Spice. There is a red food stain on his tie and a small, pink bald spot above his temple shaped like a tiny, diseased heart. The driver starts the car and the chief directs him.

"What is your name?" the man in the suit asks.

I'm so surprised he speaks English that I don't answer right away.

"Do you speak English?"

"Yes," I say. "My name is Ronald Percy."

"You are an American?"

"Yes," I say. "Yes. I don't understand what's happening. Where are they taking me? I've done nothing wrong. I only came to report a crime."

"Speak slowly," the man says.

I repeat myself. This time I speak more slowly. "What is going on?"

"We are waiting for more information. We must bottle you until we get it."

"What information? How long? This is a mistake. All I did was—"

The man holds up his hand. "I know only that you must be bottled."

"Bottled? What does that mean?"

"Only that you will be bottled."

"How long will I be bottled?"

"Until they gather the information."

"But what information? All I did was report a crime."

"That is all I can tell you."

"I would like to speak to someone from the embassy."

"That is not possible."

"That is my right." My voice is rising in pitch. I want to take him by the shoulders and shake him.

"You have no right," he says, his voice suddenly becoming vicious. "You must stop talking."

The car stops in front of a large stone building. The man says something to the chief and they shake hands. The chief touches his forehead to the other man's wrist.

"Please," the man in the suit says, his voice calm once more, "follow me."

The building is cool and damp inside. There is a small foyer with a door at its rear that leads onto a hallway. The floor is littered with cigarette butts. A man sleeps against one wall with his hands beneath his head. He is dressed in red polyester pants and an ancient New Orleans Saints T-shirt. The man in the suit kicks the sleeping man as we pass and hisses out a command. The sleeper jumps to his feet and rushes out the door and into the waning sunlight. I am envious.

We pass through the second doorway and into a narrow hall. At its conclusion, water drips from the ceiling into a gray plastic bucket.

"Where are we going?" I ask.

"We are going to the Donkey Room."

This Donkey Room looks much the same as the last one. He seats me at a table and leaves the room, locking the door behind him, only to return minutes later with another man in a shoddy black suit. They sit across the table from me and speak to each other in Amharic for several minutes.

Finally, the new man looks me over and says, "How many corn do you have?"

"Do not lie," the first man says. "You will be caught and then it will be serious."

I lie. "Five hundred dollars."

"Please give us the corn and your passport."

I pull up my shirt and unfasten my money belt. It feels as though several days have passed since I put it on this morning. I empty it onto the table. There are ten fifty dollar bills, a thumb width wad of 100 Birr notes, my address book, my passport, and my two ADO identification cards. The room is very hot. My whole body is greasy with sweat. The two men count the money and examine my identification. The first suit says something, and the second one grunts in response, picking up my address book and flipping through its pages.

"Also, give me your watch," the second one says.

I hand it over. It is a cheap plastic Timex, but I am sorry to see it go. My official identity has been taken from me and now I have lost time, too.

"You are a member of the CIA," the second man says. It is almost phrased as a question but not quite.

"No, I am not a member of the CIA."

"It will only go bad if you persist in lying," he says.

"I'm not lying. Call the embassy."

They both laugh at this, and then confer among themselves for almost fifteen minutes. The first suit seems to be arguing for some plan of action. The second suit nods and occasionally interjects a comment. Finally, they arrive at a conclusion and stop talking.

"Can someone please tell me what is going on?" I say.

"Do not talk," the first suit says. He barely moves his lips when he speaks.

"The man you should be looking for is Dr. Cavarri," I say, hoping this will provoke a response. It does.

The second suit slaps the tabletop between us. The sound echoes in the small room. I lurch backwards and wince in surprise. He shouts, pressing my sternum with his forefinger. "If you talk again, I will kick you."

They discuss something heatedly. Both of them seem to be upset, but it is impossible to determine whether they are displeased with each other or with the problem I have caused them. The second suit pounds his fist on the table. They are silent for a moment and then the first suit stands abruptly and leaves. The second suit picks up my money and identification and follows him.

"Where are you going?" I ask as they leave.

The door clicks shut and a deadbolt slides into place.

15

I am asleep when the door opens again. I have absolutely no idea what time it is or how long I've been in the room. I don't even remember drifting off to sleep. Two soldiers enter and motion for me to follow them. I'm stupid with drowsiness. Outside it is night, but which night? I climb into a transport truck that has been painted with a tiger stripe camouflage design. I am too tired to attempt communicat-

ing with the soldiers and they do not seem to care one way
or the other. We drive along a tree-lined road in silence.
Insects thicken the beams of the headlights and collect on
the windshield in greasy, yellow clumps. We do not travel
far, no more than five miles. When we stop, it is at the edge
of a fenced enclosure topped with concertina wire. There is
a strong smell of urine. The soldiers hand me over to another
set of soldiers who lead me through a small door in the
gate. I must duck to get in. And then I am pushed through
another small door beside a set of wooden steps leading up
to a guard tower. The smell of piss is even stronger now and
it is mixed with the smell of rank sweat and excrement. On
the other side of the second door, there is a large open area
enclosed by a ragged wall made from large pieces of galvanized steel roofing. In the dark it is difficult to gauge, but it
looks about the size of a basketball court. It is filled with a
hundred or so men huddled in small groups. Their combined
voices sound like the murmuring of night insects. In the far
corner, a fire is burning. Sparks pour up into the sky like
novice stars. The glare of the fire distorts the faces of the
men who sit beside it, making them appear ghoulish and
inhuman. The steel door slams shut behind me. A bolt slides
into place with a terrific clang. Several men look up at the
sound of the metal clanking, but it is only with the mildest
of curiosity. No one speaks to me. I find an empty spot
along the wall and sit down. My back aches from sleeping
in a chair. I pull my knees up to my chin and close my eyes.
The last of my money presses against the inside of my
thigh. It is not over yet, I think. As long as I have this
money, it is not over.

16

The detention yard is no longer mysterious or sinister in the washed out pastels of early morning, only depressing. The yard is smaller than I thought and there are fewer men. My fellow inmates seem completely indifferent to my presence, but I have no doubt I'm watched closely. Although I never see anyone looking at me directly, I feel as though I am being scrutinized. Sized up for possible worth or advantage. As the sun gets higher, the men drift into groups that move in slow counterclockwise circles around the edge of the prison yard. There are no trees. There is no shade of any kind. Only the sun and the piss-watered dust and the smell of a large group of unwashed men.

I watch them walk for several hours before I feel compelled to stand and join them. The motion is compulsive and pointless, but also it is somehow soothing. In a place where there is nothing, this is something. Something small, but something nonetheless.

17

The latrines are shallow, open pits with two precariously balanced boards on which to squat. There are two of them.

One is full and almost impossible to use without being splattered. The other is on a slight incline, and it is very easy to slip off of it. On the second morning, I see a man slip and fall into the pit. When he re-emerges, dripping with a wet coat of liquid shit, no one will speak to him. By the end of the day, he is openly weeping. He walks from group to group trying to start a conversation, but as soon he approaches, men flee. During the night, he screams a single word over and over again until a group of men fall upon him and kick him into silence. They will not touch him with their hands. The next morning he sits with his back against the wall pounding his head with a small rock. He isn't hitting himself very hard, but it doesn't take long before he is covered in blood as well as shit. On the third morning he is openly taunting the guards. I don't understand what he's saying, but it becomes quickly apparent why he's doing what he's doing. At dusk, he screams at the guards and attempts to scale the fence. It's over quickly. The bullet enters the back of his head and tears off his face. The guards conscript three men to drag him out. Even dead, the men want nothing to do with him. It is not until one prisoner is struck in the head with the butt of a rifle that those chosen will do the job.

18

Twice a day we are given water and a piece of stale *injera*. *Injera* has almost no nutritional value and the water we are given is the colour of café au lait. No one can last long on this diet. Even the healthiest of men must begin to deteriorate after a couple of weeks. Some men have relatives who live nearby. During mealtimes, a crowd forms outside the fence and food and other necessities are passed through. The only other way to supplement one's diet is to bribe the guards. In addition to the bribe, there is at least a one hundred percent mark-up, usually more.

It is not difficult to judge the amount of time a man has spent here. It is measured as much in body weight, remaining teeth and the expression of the eyes as it is in time served. There are twenty-year-old men shuffling around in the bodies of sixty-year-olds.

The first two days I do not drink the water. I am certain I'll become ill as soon as I do, but I also worry about taking out my money and spending it on food. Once I start, it will be gone quickly and then I'll have nothing to fall back on. Or it will be stolen once it is known that I have it. I'm convinced I can use the money more wisely, but there is no one here who speaks English and the bribe I'd need to make requires subtle negotiating. I wait for an opportunity.

19

I drink the water. I wake up puking. I cannot control my bowels. I can barely walk. The fever makes me delusional and I believe for a time that I'm involved in a life and death game of baseball. The other prisoners are my teammates and foes.

The fact there is no ball in play does not disturb my fever logic. We are all just running bases. I drink more water, because if I don't I'll become dehydrated and die. The world is a patch of packed earth four feet long and four feet wide. The end of my toe is as far away as my childhood home in Savannah. Things happen to me. Someone kicks me in the head. I lose my eye and panic, but then find it again almost immediately. I shake as though I have just avoided death. I drink the water. I sweat in the sun. I tremble. I vomit. I piss out of my ass. I drink the water.

20

On the day they come for us, I am still weak, but the worst has passed. Since becoming sick, I've completely lost track of time. I don't know how long I've been here. I can't think clearly. My thoughts break up inside my head before they form. Sentences trail off. It occurs to me that I could die; however, the thought has lost much of its power. I feel dead already. Or at least sub-human. I can no longer communicate. I must look as though I'm losing the struggle because the men around me do not acknowledge my existence anymore. During the first days, I was allowed to walk with certain groups of men even though we could not speak to one another. Now any group I attempt to join dissolves upon my approach. I have seen it with others. If you look like you're about to die, no one wants to be around you. They might catch it themselves.

The soldiers come in the afternoon. They choose fifteen of us. There doesn't seem to be any logical pattern to their selection. Our hands are bound behind our backs and we are blindfolded with burlap rags. Then we are loaded onto some kind of vehicle. None of the men speak. The engine coughs into life and the truck shudders. Soon we are moving over a rough track. Men fall against each other. The floor comes up suddenly and slaps you in unexpected places. Two men beside me kick each other and scream. The road flattens out. The truck is hot when we climb in, but it becomes hotter and hotter. It is increasingly difficult to breathe. Some of the healthier men who still have the energy to panic do. They shout at God and the soldiers.

Time passes and the only sound is the men beside me gasping and coughing like consumptives. The constant grind of the engine. I feel myself fading off. Whether I'm going for good or just going to sleep I don't know. Either way, fighting it now is just a waste of oxygen and energy. I think about the eye the doctors removed as I drift off. I wonder where it is. What do they do with the parts of people they remove? The hands, the legs, the diseased lungs, the eyes? It has probably been incinerated or piled in some special dump for medical waste, where perhaps it has found its way into the belly of a crow. Maybe my eye has been converted to feathers and is at this very moment flying along the coast of Georgia.

21

The door swings open and the air that comes in is cold and dry. A wind whips around the outside of the truck. My tongue is thick and coated with sticky dust. My left arm has gone to sleep and my right arm burns and tingles. I try to squeeze my hands and pump some blood back through, but my left hand has become nerveless meat. The soldiers shout and bang on the truck with sticks. While trying to get out, I trip and fall and someone kicks me in the kidney. My blindfold slides up for a second. We are in the desert. The sun is rising. I see a gas station sign. I scramble around like a crab on its back until a soldier yanks me up by my dead arm. The blindfold falls back in place. Someone pushes me forward and I almost trip again, but I catch my balance just in time. I feel the spray of the man next to me taking a piss and I move aside. Someone else is not so quick. A blind fight ensues and I get a smack on the side of the head. One of the soldiers fires off a couple of rounds and the fighting stops.

We are loaded onto a bigger vehicle with new prisoners. My teeth chatter. I am glad when another prisoner is pushed down beside me. It is warmer. When the man lands, he says, shit. He's neither American nor English. His accent is African. And I hope for a second it's not just a word learned from a Jean Claude VanDamme movie, but it's stupid to think there is someone on this truck who can speak English, so I put it out of my head. Hoping can sometimes make things worse. You just have to concentrate on getting from one hour to the next. Thinking about anything more is deadly.

This truck is better ventilated, but the result is that dust comes in with the air. It is painful to breathe. The truck heats up as the sun rises. Someone in front of me falls on my foot and twists my ankle. There's no damage done, but it hurts and I say, goddamnit.

"What?" the man next to me says.

"Yes?" I say.

"You speak English?" the man says.

"I do."

"You're an American?"

"I am."

"This is very good," the man says. "Talking English makes me feel better."

I feel more than better. I feel human. I don't know how long it's been since I spoke English. It seems like a month, but I'm sure that's not true.

"What is your name?" he says.

"Ronald."

"Ronald. That is a good name. I am Dr. Tesfaye."

"Dr. Tesfaye," I say, almost out of my head with gratitude.

"Let me do something for you, Ato Ronald."

"What?"

"Turn your back to me and I'll loosen your ropes. Mine weren't tied very well and I can slip them on and off."

I edge around, accidentally kicking the man in front of

me and making him yell. Dr. Tesfaye's fingers pull and loosen until I can slip my right hand free. The left is still dead, but my relief is immediate. I reach up to take off my blindfold. Dr. Tesfaye stops me.

"There's a guard on either end of the truck. If they see you've loosened your rope, they will kick you horribly."

Slowly, blood comes back into my numb arm. It stings. "Thank you," I say. I'm so grateful I feel as though I could cry. My eye burns from the dust and held back tears. I need to clean my empty socket. Sand and grit have gotten behind my glass eye. Every time I move my face it grinds at the skin there. It feels raw.

"Are you hungry?" he asks.

"Yes."

"Slide your hand over."

He places three smooth objects the size of Brazil nuts into my palm. I do not hesitate. I put them in my mouth and crunch. They are locusts with their legs removed. Hunger has shaped my taste to include anything digestible.

"How did you get bottled?" he says.

"I don't know exactly. I haven't understood what's been happening to me for the past few weeks. I found a dead body and I reported it to the police and now I'm here."

Dr. Tesfaye makes a sympathetic noise.

"What about you?" I say.

"I will never know for certain, but I believe someone reported that I was a member of the Oromo Liberation Front. One night they came to my house and took me away. My wife and children were not there when they bearded me. They have no idea where I am. That is what makes me feel the worst. They do not know. It would be better if they thought I was dead."

"Bearded?"

"It is when someone accuses you falsely of holding radical political beliefs."

"Do you know who—"

"Yes," he says and he sounds so disgusted that I don't say anything for a few moments.

"I was a college professor and physician. I applied for a position in the Anatomy Department at Addis Abeba University at the same time as another colleague. He was competitive. He bragged that they would choose him over me. After I was told I had been given the position, I made the mistake of telling a friend before it was publicly announced. This friend threw me a party to celebrate and spread the news to all our other colleagues. The very next night they came for me. This is the only explanation that makes sense."

"God," I say, "is it that easy to send a man to jail?"

"It's nothing to send a man to jail. I'm lucky to be alive."

The truck bounces. The man on the other side of me moans. I squeeze both hands. My arm feels normal again.

"You know, my friend, we are not going to a jail."

"What do you mean?"

"We are going to a work camp."

"Is there a difference?"

"The difference is, you don't come back from a work camp."

The guard shouts at us and pounds his rifle butt against the floor of the truck.

"We must be quiet," Dr. Tesfaye says. "This is a bad man, this guard. I saw him beat a boy almost to death for urinating on himself."

"There will be time to talk."

"I hope so."

22

I cannot see for several moments after they remove the blindfold. We are in the middle of a wasteland of dry thorn bushes and jagged rocks. There is nothing visible in any direction except for the work camp. They line us up outside the gate and tell us to remove our clothes. There are twenty of us, including the old man who died on the trip here. His body is laid out on the rocks in front of us. He wears a rigor mortis grin that makes him look like he would bite us if he could. One of the guards removes his shoes and pants. He tries to take the dead man's shirt, but it comes apart in his fingers.

Dr. Tesfaye stands beside me. He is a tall man with a large frame and hair cut close to the scalp. He has a scar on his chin in the shape of a star. He wears a small, neat mustache. After my eye adjusts to the light, we shake hands and he tells me we must stick together. We might have a chance if we work as a team. When he smiles, he looks the way I imagined him to while blindfolded.

The guards here are much more thorough in their search than those in town. We are told to take off our clothes. Each man is required to bend over and spread the cheeks of his ass apart. A teenage boy, two men down from me, is discovered to be hiding a wad of one hundred Birr notes in his ass. The money is confiscated and he is pushed down and kicked. My throat is so dry it makes a clicking sound when I swallow. I swallow and swallow. I can't seem to stop myself. The sound becomes louder the longer I do it. Dr. Tesfaye nudges me and gives me a look. My esophagus feels as though it's fusing shut.

The guard discovers my money almost immediately. The man lets out a whoop and holds the bills up in the air. Another guard hurries over to take a look. The first guard rushes off, still holding the bills in the air. He brings yet another guard back with him. A huge man with biceps the size of my thighs. He stands in front of me for a moment. I am careful not to look him in the eye. The wind moves the sand at my feet. Somewhere in the work camp, a man is shouting. The new guard grabs my chin and lifts my face up.

"Motherfucker," he says, "motherfucker, motherfucker, motherfucker." He says it lovingly, but his eyes are hard. He clears his throat, spits a gobbet of mucus the size of a fried egg onto my face and then saunters back to the guardhouse beside the gate. I do not wipe the spit off because the other two guards are watching me. I get the feeling they are waiting for any excuse to beat the shit out of me. I don't give them an excuse.

We are instructed to dress again, but neither my pants nor my underwear are returned to me. I am so filled up with anguish and frustration I feel like I'm walking underwater. For a moment I think I might lose consciousness, but it passes.

"Do not worry, my friend," Dr. Tesfaye whispers, "we will find you some trousers."

23

The gate to the work camp is a flimsy-looking sheet of galvanized steel, rusting and torn. It is not even attached in a permanent way, merely propped up against two posts. On either side is a small windowless guardhouse. One is empty and in the other a man sits and smokes with his rifle laying across his knees. The fence surrounding the work camp is constructed from ten-foot concrete posts strung together with a dozen or so strands of thin wire carrying a high voltage current. The hum is clearly audible from fifteen yards away. From the sound of it, the current might be strong enough to kill. At intervals along the fence there are small guardhouses. It would be nothing to slip out, as most of the guardhouses look unoccupied, but in this place, high security precautions are unnecessary because the desert acts as a prison wall. Even if an escaping prisoner did manage to take water and food along with him, the landscape is flat and featureless. There is nowhere to hide.

We are marched through the gate past the guards' quarters and mess hall, a row of one-storey cinder block buildings painted the colour of eggplant, and what looks like an administrative building. In the distance ahead, there is the sound of heavy machinery pounding the earth, and the sky at the horizon is stained yellow from the raised dust. This end of the prison camp is deserted. The sun is unrelenting. We walk about a kilometre along a dirt road lined with waist-high cactus growing so closely together they form a natural fence. Then there is a turnoff, which leads to another group of cinder block buildings. These are much larger, but also painted purple. We are led into the first of these buildings. The number seven is painted above the door in white. The building is filled with pieces of machinery. At the far end there are six large trucks. One is a fuel truck. It has been recently painted, but the Exxon logo is still clearly visible. Along the wall nearest the door are six or seven long tables. Guards are milling around each one. Some with AK-47s, some without. We are ushered one by one to each table. I lead the way.

At the first table, a man in a blue smock gives me a physical examination. He inspects my ears and nose and mouth, using a penlight. It has been twelve hours since I last took a piss. As soon as I think about it, I can't imagine waiting another moment. I shift my weight from foot to foot. He listens to my chest with a battered stethoscope, feels the muscles on my thighs and arms and scribbles the results of his examination on the notepad in front of him. I'm curious to see what conclusions he has drawn about the state of my health, but the notations are written using the Ge'ez alphabet. He tears the sheet off the notepad and hands it to me. I move on to the next table. This man simply looks at me for a moment, writes a note on my paper, and I am passed along again, where a third man removes the cheap silver ring I wear on my pinkie and tosses it into a wooden crate on the floor. The crate is filled with shoddy jewelry and eyeglasses and what looks like a toupee, but I can't be sure about the toupee because I'm prodded along with the barrel of an AK-47. At the last table, a man wearing a scarlet beret looks at my paper and compares it with a list on a clipboard beside him. He says something to an older man with graying hair at the other end of the table, who is seated next to a rack of thin wooden rods. This man takes my paper and directs me to sit on a folding metal chair. On the floor next to him, a small campstove is burning. Two guards come and stand on either side of me. The man behind the table selects one of the rods from the rack. A short length of wire with an intricate metal stamp protrudes from the end of the rod. He places this in the flame of the campstove and smiles at me. He says something to the men standing beside me and they laugh. When the rod is removed from the flame, its tip is glowing orange. One of the guards yanks up my sleeve, tearing the rotten material of my shirt, and takes hold of my arm with both hands. The other guard grips my shoulders and leans against me. I close my eye. There is a slight pop and a sizzling sound. I smell roast pork and then I piss all over myself.

24

"I thought they were going to kill you," Dr. Tesfaye says.
    "So did I," I say.
He examines my mouth. My left incisor has been broken in half by a rifle butt and I think I may have a cracked rib. I

have a headache that makes my vision blurry. We have been separated into groups of two and three, determined by our work assignments. The branding designates both our duties and living quarters. Dr. Tesfaye and I are lucky enough to get the same brand. It is the Ge'ez character signifying the sound "doe."

"Here," Dr. Tesfaye hands me my eye, "this fell out when they beat you. Luckily, they didn't notice it. They probably would not have given it back to you."

"Thanks." I put it in the pocket of my shirt. "Where do they have us working?"

While I was unconscious, each group's working duties were explained. As we talk, the other men are herded out. We are the last ones left. I feel strangely calm, as though the anxiety was beaten out of me along with some blood and a portion of my tooth. My branded arm throbs.

"They have not told us."

"That doesn't sound good."

Dr. Tesfaye shrugs.

"What kind of work did the others get?"

"Working in different mine shafts."

"Jesus," I say.

"I've heard rumors about this camp."

"Like what?"

"That this is a uranium mine."

"I didn't know there was uranium in Ethiopia."

The door opens, letting in a shaft of bright, white light. The two guards slumped beside it stand up straight. The guard behind us yanks us to our feet. All I can see is a dark shape at first, which slowly takes on definition and becomes two men. The first is a guard and the second is a prisoner. All of the guards have begun to blur together in my head. They are just uniforms. I never look directly into their faces. I stare at a place ten feet behind them when they speak to me. The prisoner who comes in with the guard looks surprisingly healthy. He is round-faced and plump and smiles at me while the guard speaks to Dr. Tesfaye in rapid, clipped Amharic. Dr. Tesfaye occasionally nods his head and says, *ow*, which means yes. As quickly as he comes in, the guard leaves and it is just the three of us walking out of the building and down the road. It is the first time I have been unsupervised since I reported the dead body.

The plump prisoner is Melaku. He oversees the kitchens at the work camp. We will be working under him. He has a loud, pleasant laugh and he uses it a lot as we walk to the kitchens. He pats me on the back and smiles several times.

"This is good," Dr. Tesfaye says. "We will not starve now."

25

The kitchens are vile. They are housed in a shell of a building that was hit by an artillery shell during the war with Somalia. The walls are made of cinder blocks and the roof is made from pieces of canvas sheeting sewn together. The canvas is tied down to stakes around the walls to keep it from blowing away. In some places the walls lean in at such a pitch it looks as though they might fall at any moment. There are no doors or panes of glass in the windows. Inside,

the floors are caked an inch thick with trampled refuse from
the stoves. Flies cover everything like a sticky black liquid
and the smoke from the cooking fires hangs in the air at
shoulder level. There are ten fires going at once, each one
heating a large metal pot. A short man with a limp walks
from pot to pot, stirring them with a wooden plank. He is
stripped to the waist and shiny with sweat. It is fifteen
degrees hotter in the kitchen than it is outside. The heat
sucks the air out of my lungs.

"Could the mines be much worse than this?" I say.

"Yes," Dr. Tesfaye says, nodding his head emphatically.

Melaku points to various things in the kitchen and speaks
in a cheerful voice. We stop in the middle of the room and
he looks me over. It seems as though he has just now
noticed I am not wearing pants. He frowns, says something
to Dr. Tesfaye and goes outside.

"He says he will try and find you some trousers, but in
the meantime he's going to get something for you to wear."

Melaku reappears with a large, woven jute bag that once
held potatoes. Using the fingernail on his index finger,
which is long and blackened, he slits holes for my arms and
head. He hands it to me with both hands as though offer-
ing me a platter and I slip it over my head. It comes down
to my knees, covering everything important except my urine
stained socks.

"How do you say thank you?" I ask Dr. Tesfaye.

"*Amasayganalow*," he says, and I do my best to repeat the
word to Melaku.

"Where do the prisoners eat?" I ask Melaku through Dr.
Tesfaye.

"In the mines," he says. "They never leave the earth."

Melaku tells us that we may sleep on the floor of the kitchen or outside in the yard if we like and that he will try to find something for us to wrap ourselves in on cold nights. He leads us to a waist-high mound of half-rotted greens of some kind and tells us to chop them into inch long strips. We don't see him again until it is time to take the food to the mines.

26

As soon as he turns his back, we gorge ourselves on the gritty, bitter leaves. Food has never been so satisfying. Dr. Tesfaye's face is smeared with juice. My hands are stained green. The other kitchen worker watches, but he says nothing.

"What is the last thing you ate?" I ask Dr. Tesfaye.

"Locust."

"Me, too."

The other kitchen worker hobbles over. He is missing a foot and has a red plastic cup tied over his stump to protect it. He says something to Dr. Tesfaye in a gruff voice and then goes back to stirring pots.

"What did he say?"

"His name is Yonas. He says that we will make ourselves sick if we continue eating the raw leaves."

"Maybe we should stop," I say.

"Yes, that is a good idea."

But we don't. There is so much food here right now.
Who knows if we'll have food tomorrow? After a while the
greens stop tasting as delicious as they did at first. Still, we
keep on eating. The leaves feel like a sack of marbles in my
belly. I bite down on a pebble and my broken tooth throbs
with a pain so sharp it astonishes me. I make a muffled
yelping sound and almost choke. We continue stuffing ourselves.

"I can't eat any more," Dr. Tesfaye says, shoving a leaf in
his mouth.

"Me neither."

"We will eat one more leaf only and then stop," Dr.
Tesfaye says.

"You're right," I say.

Two leaves later I feel the first rumble in my stomach. Dr.
Tesfaye has stopped eating for the first time in the last half
hour. His face looks ashy.

"I am feeling the ill will of these leaves," Dr. Tesfaye says.
"They are angry leaves."

"I'm feeling poorly as—"

Dr. Tesfaye jumps up and runs to the door. I follow close
behind. Just knowing what he is about to do has triggered
a similar reaction in my own belly. By the time I catch up
with him, he is puking thick ropes of masticated leaf. I dou-
ble over and do the same.

"I am vomiting, Ronald. I am vomiting," Dr. Tesfaye says
between heaves. He sounds inordinately disturbed to discover
this.

"What a waste," I say. My hair is wet with sweat.

When I look up, Yonas is standing in the doorway. He is

laughing so hard he is holding his belly, as if to contain these powerful laughs, but he is absolutely silent. Dr. Tesfaye says something to him, but Yonas just waves him away with his hand and goes back into the kitchen.

27

From above ground, the mines don't look like much. The first thing one sees when approaching them is a small mountain made of dirt and mining by-products and castoff machinery. It must be the highest point for fifty miles. It has the circumference of a city block and stands about three storeys high. Beside it is the ore crushing machine. Ore comes up out of the earth and is dumped onto a conveyer belt, which takes the watermelon-sized clumps of yellow rock up to the chute and drops them into the maw of the machine, where heavy iron plates smash it into smaller bits. These bits are then loaded onto trucks and taken who knows where. It is the loudest piece of machinery I have ever been exposed to. When it is running, you cannot hear a spoken word within a hundred yards, and even then, one must scream in order to make oneself heard. The ground vibrates around it so much that anything smaller than a wheelbarrow literally bounces into the air each time a crushing plate comes down.

In order to bring the food to the miners, we must be lowered by hand down a shaft the height of a five-storey building. The diesel generator, which usually operates it, is broken. Now there is only a metal bucket with room for four, a pulley and a thick rope. It takes six men to lower us into the hole. The four of us—Melaku, Yonas, Dr. Tesfaye and myself—go down one at a time, each sharing the bucket with two huge dented aluminum pots of food. The food consists of two kinds of stew. Red stew and green stew. It doesn't smell bad, but I find it is impossible to determine the ingredients, even after eating considerable portions of each. When I ask Yonas, he tells me that green and yellow things go in the green stew and red and brown things go in the red stew.

Once the stew is transported into the mine, the pots are loaded onto mine carts and wheeled for what seems like a half mile. The tunnels nearest to the entrance are lit with electricity, but the further we move from the entrance, the more primitive the lighting becomes. By the time we reach the eating area, which looks like it could be the mead drinking hall in *Beowulf*, the passageway is lit by torches made from green sticks wrapped in burlap and dipped in tar or creosote. They produce a great quantity of foul-smelling smoke.

The miners are impatient. They shout when they see us. Guards must fend them off or we would be overrun in minutes. One miner breaks through the line of guards and grabs a hold of my pot, almost tipping it over. The nearest guard is holding a torch. He hits the miner on the head with it. Whatever it is that is soaking the cloth as fuel rubs off on the miner's hair. He runs back into the crowd of men, screaming in a frightening, high-pitched voice, his head flaming. It is the voice of a terrified teenage girl, but it comes from the body of a work wizened gnome. Another guard fires a burst of rounds over the heads of the miners and they settle down a little. The rounds ricochet. One of the miners near me is grazed on the cheek.

Our job is to ladle stew. A ragged queue forms and the miners march past with outstretched plastic bowls. The bowls are connected to the miners pants by a length of cord. Their faces are yellow with dust and their eyes are an angry red, like actors in a Kabuki performance. Each one watches closely to make certain they get a fair portion. If they feel shorted, they pour their stew back in the pot and hold out their bowl again. One man does this to me three times in a row, which I don't understand because I am pouring as much as the bowl will hold. A guard watches this unfold. The third time the miner does this, the guard produces an aerosol canister from a pocket in his shirt and sprays him in the face with something orange. The miner screams and stumbles backwards into the swarm of men. It looks as though the other miners are beating him, but all I can make out for certain are his muffled shouts. And these don't last long. Once the men get their bowl of stew, they leave the eating room and disappear back into the mines.

There are about thirty men left in line when we run out of stew. One of the miners falls to his knees and begins to cry when he discovers there is no food. Yonas tells us this happens every night and some of the weaker miners never get to eat at all. This explains their ferocious behaviour when we arrived.

28

A new truckload of prisoners comes at least once every two weeks, sometimes more frequently. I've seen them arrive twice now. Each truck has twenty or so men and they follow the same ritual we went through when they arrive. They are lined up and strip-searched outside the gates of the camp. A few of them are beaten, just to get them in the spirit of things here, I guess. The beatings are random. Any minor difficulty will bring a stick down on your head. Then they are taken into the processing building and given a brand and a work assignment. Their arrival brings out something ugly in me. I don't quite understand. I resent them, the newcomers. Whenever a truck carrying new prisoners rolls in, I feel angry and agitated. I get a perverse satisfaction from seeing them beaten. It scares me and makes me feel depressed. Where did this come from? I'm just under duress, I tell myself. This isn't me, I tell myself. But it is. What will I be like in a year? Two years? Already I'm no better than a goat. Eating whatever filth I can find, shitting in the bushes, taking pleasure from the misery of the other poor fucks around me.

29

"How can those mines hold so many men?" I ask Yonas. "A truck came in this morning with at least thirty men. There can't be any room down there. And it always seems like we feed about the same amount of people."

Dr. Tesfaye and I are bringing in water from the muddy well behind the kitchen, bucket by bucket. Yonas stirs it into the stew with a two-by-four and directs water to certain pots. Since we arrived, he has contracted a skin disease of some kind. The skin on his arms and chest is sloughing off in three-inch strips. The skin on his face and in his armpits has dried and cracked into fish scales. The sores are septic and suppurating. Dr. Tesfaye blended together an ointment made of red clay and mutton fat and plants he found growing in the ditch behind the enlisted men's latrines. Yonas smears this all over his upper body every morning. It looks as though it may be working, but his skin is very slow to heal. In the flickering light of the smoky cooking fires and with red mud smeared all over his chest and face, Yonas looks like some kind of bush shaman stirring up a magic concoction with his two-by-four.

Yonas doesn't respond to Dr. Tesfaye's translation. He just looks at me as though I'm mentally defective or hopelessly ignorant, which I suppose I am. Since the fever I contracted in the first holding camp, I've felt disoriented and confused.

I have a hard time following thoughts to their logical conclusion. My mind skitters off track. I can't even daydream
properly. My fantasy imaginings of escape and revenge get
lost and confused before they've even begun. I start out
thinking about how to get under the electrified fence and
end up staring blankly at a fly on my wrist. And I won't
even remember when I veered off. I'm unsettled.

A half hour later Yonas answers my question.

"I'll show you after we feed the miners," he tells Dr.
Tesfaye.

"Do you know?" I ask Dr. Tesfaye when he tells me.

"No," Dr. Tesfaye says. "I also have asked myself that
question."

30

"Where are we going?" I ask, but Yonas doesn't respond. Dr.
Tesfaye and I exchange looks. We're worried about being
seen by the guards and what they will do to punish us.
What happened in the mines during dinner today has made
us gloomy. I can see it in his face although we have not
spoken about it.

Yonas leads us around the three-storey mound of mine
refuse and dirt. The end of the day has turned the world
lavender. A wind is sweeping across the desert and the air is
cool. There is sand between my teeth, which crunches each
time I bring my jaws together. A bit of grit has lodged behind
my glass eye and no amount of cleaning will get it out. The

socket feels raw. Behind the mound there is an empty expanse of rocky ground, flat and barren. The only thing that breaks the monotony of the landscape is the perimeter fence in the far distance. One of the guardhouses is occupied. A small campfire in front of it shudders in the wind. Sparks whoosh into the darkening desert. We follow a path of packed clay. The foot traffic has cleared the sand and polished the earth so it shines with the reflection of the setting sun.

Several hundred yards behind the mound is another entrance to the mine. Instead of plunging straight down into the earth, as the two other entrances do, this one has been carved into the earth at a slight slant. It looks much older. Inside there are torches flickering and voices.

"It's the dead mine," Yonas says.

Two prisoners pushing an ore cart come out of the shaft, followed by guards with guns. The prisoners are singing.

"What are they singing?" I ask Dr. Tesfaye.

"I don't know it," he says, "but it is about God."

They pass us without a greeting or, even more surprisingly in the case of the guards, without an ugly look. I wonder for a moment if they did not see us, but this could not possibly be the case as they came within feet of us.

Yonas says something to Dr. Tesfaye.

"He says to shout hello to the guards," Dr. Tesfaye says.

"Fuck no," I say. This could easily be cause for a beating.

Yonas yells several Amharic curses: 'cat face,' 'skull full of snot,' 'fucker of goats'. I get ready to run, but the guards do not acknowledge it. I look back and forth between Yonas and Dr. Tesfaye. Yonas is laughing his silent laugh, holding his belly with both hands. Dr. Tesfaye looks appalled.

"They will not speak until they pass the mound," Yonas says.

"Why?" I ask.

"Ghosts," Yonas says.

We walk into the mouth of the mine and I can smell it right away. I know this smell. This smell is the cause of all my present problems. It no longer makes me gag. We continue into the mine. The sun has disappeared. We are almost out of light. A torch burns a little further in. In its flickering light, I can see the bodies. Hundreds of them stacked like cords of wood. Jesus. I back out quickly and Yonas laughs.

"This is where they go," Yonas says. "There are more people stacked here than have lived in my village for a hundred years."

31

The days are blending into one big day, punctuated only by the occasional act of violence. And now that I have been here for a while, even this does nothing to distinguish one day from the next. Dr. Tesfaye believes we have been here for three months, but I do not think we have been here that long. After our discussion about this, we keep track by scratching an X in the lintel of the kitchen door each morning. The X's collect quickly and I wonder if he may not be right about the time. I feel as though I have always been here and it worries me to think what that may mean. My life is being devoured before my eyes.

Our daily schedule almost never changes. We wake at

dawn and eat the food we hoarded and hid from the night before. Sometimes Melaku will share the coffee grounds he steals from the enlisted men's mess hall, where he is the sole cook. Most days he does not. There is a guard who keeps an inventory of the food in the enlisted men's kitchen. Melaku is only allowed to take refuse and spoilage.

After our desultory breakfast, we walk the half-mile to the guards' quarters and start a fire using the wood from the packing crates the machinery is shipped in. The aluminum laundry pots are set to boil. If there is no one around, we use this water to wash ourselves before we put the clothes in. While the water warms, we go to the officers' houses and collect their dirty clothes. The enlisted men do not get this service, and as a result, they seldom wash their clothes. Women are not allowed in the camp, and because of this, the officers select prisoners to be their maids. These men are referred to as Fantas, after the sickly sweet soft drink, since it is assumed that they function as females in other regards as well. The nearest town large enough to have prostitutes is almost eight hours away. The Fantas have a tendency to be bitchy and overly particular, probably because they will be blamed if the laundry comes out wrong; but they also have the highest status among the prisoners and the most comfortable life, so they look down on the rest of us. Not surprisingly, they are hated in return. They give us the dirty clothes wrapped in bedding and occasionally a tidbit of gossip. It is the Fantas who teach me the most interesting Amharic words.

Once the laundry is collected, we bring it back and boil it for a couple of hours, put it out on the laundry lines, and

then fold it and return it when it has dried. If food has
been delivered, we pick it up at the gate and spend the
afternoon chopping. Anything and everything goes into the
stew. Although they are mainly comprised of cloudy, yellow
water pumped up from the well behind the kitchen, the
scrapings off the enlisted men's dishes are the nutritional
base of every stew. Then come beans or lentils if they are
available. Next, we add fresh vegetables when they are allot-
ted, or if they are not, the rotting vegetables left over from
the enlisted men's kitchen. On Sundays we get to use the
grease and bones from the enlisted men's roasted mutton.
This is the highlight of our week. The four of us sit around
the kitchen gnawing the last bits of flesh and gristle from
the bones, relating stories from the week with grease shiny
mouths. If there is a real bounty of leftover meat, Melaku
will sometimes sing mountain love songs for us as we polish
the bones with our mouths.

There are some days when there just isn't enough food to
make the stews. On these days Melaku becomes inventive. He
knows he will have to face a violent mob of half-starved
miners if there isn't at least something, so he improvises.
Once we boiled down old, worn leather gun holsters that
had been thrown away when new ones were issued. The
result was a gluey mess, to which he then added the ink
from several red pens he found in the garbage pit behind the
administrative building, a quarter kilo of powdered chilies
from the enlisted men's kitchen, which had grown a lurid
yellow fuzz of mold, finely minced grass harvested from the
sewage ditch behind the barracks toilets and the rotten rinds
of three melons left over from a party the officers had had

the previous evening to celebrate their new holsters. The kitchen staff went hungry that night, but there were no complaints from the miners. Another day the soup is made entirely of moldy potato peelings. On one occasion we are forced to spend the afternoon collecting insects. Melaku worries he is being given less and less food for the stews because the officers know he is good at making do with almost nothing.

When the stews are finished, we eat. This is the best moment of each day. Then it is down to the mines to feed the men. By the time we return it is dark and the desert wind is up and whipping through the camp. I sleep beneath a potato sack filled with grass beside Yonas and Dr. Tesfaye. Some nights Melaku sleeps in the kitchen with us, but at least three nights a week he is somewhere else. Sometimes more. We do not know where Melaku sleeps when he is away.

32

"I think we should try to escape," I say to Dr. Tesfaye. We are stirring the laundry with a plank pried off the flatbed of an abandoned truck by the ore crusher. Sweat keeps getting into my eyes and making them sting.

Dr. Tesfaye laughs. We often joke with one another about serious things. It is the only way to talk about them.

"No, I'm serious," I say. "How old are you?"

"You know I'm 35," he says, his face becoming grim. "I don't know about—"

"I'm just talking," I say.

We're quiet for a moment. The ore crushing machine begins to pound. I can feel the vibrations through the soles of my shoes.

"It is an impossible idea," Dr. Tesfaye says. "It is fantastic for you to even say such a thing." He pokes idly at the clothing with the plank and smiles. "Look at you."

I look at myself. I am wearing a ragged, plastic sack stained with food, and my shoes are held together with twine and small lengths of wire. "What?" I say.

We laugh.

"There is not a snowman's chance for hell."

"A snowball's chance *in* hell," I say.

He ignores me. "I am completely dismayed."

"What is your daughter's name again?"

"Do not use these tricks of old on me. I see how you are trying to trick my heart. Don't do it."

"I'm sorry," I say, smiling.

We stir. The machine pounds.

"After all" he says, looking crafty. "I don't like to bring this up, but you are very white."

"What does that have to do with it?"

"See, I knew that would make you angry." He laughs.

"I'm not angry. I just don't understand what that has to do with anything."

"You will stick out like a thumb."

"Couldn't I just rub dirt on my face?" I say.

"No, no, no," he says, shaking his head. "That would not even trick a donkey."

"I could wrap my head in cloth. Many men do that here."

"You forget that this is the small problem. We will never even get to the small problem because we will never get past the big problem."

"There must be a way to get through the desert," I say.

"I will make you a list of the reasons why not."

"All right."

"Number one, water." He lifts a shirt from the water, inspects it and lets it fall back with a plop.

"We can steal two petrol cans. That's twenty litres."

"That would be very heavy."

"They'll get lighter as we go."

"I do not believe it is possible to get them," he says. "Number two, the sun. You will roast like a sheep."

"I'll wrap myself in sacks. We'll travel at night."

"Number three, there is nowhere to hide during the day. They will catch us."

"We can dig holes and hide in them and sleep during the day," I say. "I know where we can steal a shovel."

"Shovel?" He shakes his head. "That is a horrible idea. Number four, where do we go?"

"We're somewhere near Kenya. We'll just use the sun and the stars to guide us south."

He laughs and shakes his finger at me. "We don't know where we are."

"I have heard this many times," I say.

"From whom?"

"Well, Melaku," I say, knowing what the response will be.

"Melaku has the mind of a goat."

"And the Fanta named Hikmet."

"A Fanta? A Fanta? These are horrible people. I wouldn't

let them guide me to the toilet."

"They overhear all kinds of—"

"They are not intelligent enough to make sense of what they hear."

"Are you out of excuses?" I ask.

"The worst reason is the last." He smiles.

"Which is?"

"Gudjis," he says.

"Gudjis?"

"Yes, Gudjis."

"What the hell are Gudjis?" I say.

"My friend, my friend. The Gudjis are horrible. They are blood-thirsty warriors. They wander in the dark on horses looking for men they can attack and steal from them their penis."

"What?" I laugh and it makes him laugh.

"It is true," he says.

"Is this like some kind of mythological creature? Like a flying goat?"

"No, they do not fly. They are men. Just deranged men who take penises. They dry them out and make necklaces out of them."

"I don't believe you."

"You will when they dry your penis and present it to some horrible Gudji woman as a wedding gift."

I look at him dubiously, but he appears to be serious.

"I have no answer for that one," I say.

"Just as I thought."

"I'll come up with something."

"You are not joking, are you, Ronald?"

"No," I say, "I am not."

33

I am standing beside the worst stew we have ever made, waiting to go into the mines. The stew is mainly water, but Melaku, in a fit of desperation, added dirt and potatoes so rotten they gave off a smell like dirty underwear. I worry about what the miners will do when we start to ladle this boiled sewage into their bowls. I know how I would feel. If they decided to riot down there, the guards couldn't hold them all off. The guards know it, which is why they are so fast to use violence.

For some reason, the ore crushing machine roars into life. I stick my fingers in my ears, but this hardly helps. I have never been this close to it while it is in motion. The sound vibrates my heart. Usually, the machine is turned off right before the guards eat and stays off for the rest of the night. A group of men approach the conveyer belt midway between the entrance to the mine and the maw of the crusher. Three guards and four prisoners. One of the guards is Director Hailu, the warden of the work camp. He is a tall man with the build of a professional wrestler, who is always easy to spot because his uniform is lavender and his hair is oiled into long, loose ringlets. He gesticulates frantically and points at the conveyer belt. The machine is even louder than normal because it is pounding itself. There is no ore to crush, so the resulting metal on metal sound is like a church bell gone terribly wrong. At first I think Director Hailu is angry because someone has turned on the machine at this hour, but then I see that the prisoners are bound. Director Hailu removes the pistol from his holster and waves it in the faces of the bound prisoners. The guards take a hold of one of the prisoners and heave him up onto the conveyer belt. He struggles and tries to roll himself off the edge of the belt before it takes him up over the top and into the maw of the machine, but he is not fast enough. The stampers are so big that there is no sound when he is crushed, but I imagine what the sound would be like and this is worse. After witnessing the fate of the first man, the next two prisoners do not struggle, but the last man puts up a ferocious fight. It is difficult for them to even get him onto the conveyer belt. During the struggle to put him on, he manages to kick Director Hailu in the jaw. In my head, there is loud applause. A standing ovation. Hailu's face distorts with rage and he fires off a round point blank into the man's knee, which blossoms like a red carnation. His lower leg swings from a bit of white gristle and then tears loose and falls into the dust. This pacifies the prisoner long enough for them to heave him and his severed leg up onto the belt. He lies still as the shuddering rubber conveyer lifts him up toward the crusher's mouth. Just before his body tips into the machine, this last man rolls right off the conveyer belt and drops twenty feet to the ground. His leg continues on without him into the crusher. I assume the drop has killed him but when the guards come to retrieve his body, he kicks them with his remaining leg. There is not enough fight left in him to prevent them from putting him on the conveyer belt again, but once he's on it, he tosses himself back and forth to the very last moment and then he drops silently into the teeth of the machine. Sometime during all of this I make a decision without realizing it.

34

Melaku brings the new boy in and I see immediately there will be trouble. He will be a bad luck boy both to himself and all those around him. I am surprised that Melaku managed to get him at all. First, we have enough workers, and second, the boy's beauty is startling. He does not look like a boy at all. He is slim and walks on his toes in such a way that his ass switches. It is feminine somehow without being effeminate. His eyelashes are long and thick, so thick they appear to be wet. His nose is prominent and thin and his cheekbones are high. He has a long, graceful neck. He is a pickpocket. He looks about fourteen years old. We all watch him. We can't help it. It has been a long time since any of us has been with a woman. This boy is the most beautiful thing we have seen since beginning our new lives as prisoners and slaves. His name is Adane.

"I can't bear it," Dr. Tesfaye whispers to me after Melaku introduces him to us. "Something horrible will happen to him."

I nod. I wish that I had never seen him.

35

Melaku likes to show the boy off and takes him everywhere except the mines and the enlisted mess hall. Although he is proud of the boy, he is also extremely jealous. He doesn't like Adane to talk with us. Melaku sleeps in the kitchen every night now, but he and the boy sleep on the other side of the room. Sometimes in the night we hear the noises they make. I take to stuffing my ears with wet burlap each night before sleeping. I cannot afford to become attached to this boy who looks like a girl. I try to avoid him whenever possible during the day. I never allow myself to be alone with him because I know if I become involved with him in any way, I'll lose my opportunity. I'll lose my nerve. I can feel it on the most intuitive level. This is bad in every way. Already I can see Dr. Tesfaye falling prey. Whenever Adane is around, he follows the boy's every move with his eyes. He tells me that when he hears the noises Melaku makes with the boy at night, he feels like breaking things.

I've begun to prepare for our escape. I have one petrol can and I am only waiting for the right opportunity to steal the other. I have extra sacks. I have rope. It is my hope that when Dr. Tesfaye sees how prepared I am he will change his mind and come with me. But now, with this boy, I'm no longer so certain about anything.

At first Melaku does not bring him to the enlisted men's

mess hall, but eventually his pride gets the better of him. I warn him. Dr. Tesfaye warns him. Yonas warns him. He tells us we're jealous and laughs. Although he is beautiful, the boy is simple-minded. He does not understand what is happening to him. One evening Dr. Tesfaye and I warn him not to go to the mess hall. He tells Melaku what we have said to him.

When Melaku comes in swinging the stick, we are cutting up the carrot greens for the green stew. I look up just in time to block the blow with my wrist. If he had swung just a little bit harder, he would have broken my arm. Dr. Tesfaye grabs him by one arm and Yonas grabs him by the other. He screams and kicks his legs.

"I will get you for this," Melaku shouts at me.

The boy watches the commotion he has caused and smiles.

"You will have nothing to fight over if you take that boy to the mess hall," Yonas says.

"All of you," Melaku yells at us. "You will be sorry. Everyone has to sleep at some time and when you do, I will be there waiting."

"Stop this," Yonas says. Yonas has known Melaku for several years and they are friends, but Melaku pays no attention.

"Remember what I said," Melaku says, keeping his eyes on me when he says it. He and the boy leave to go to the enlisted men's mess hall. The rest of us look at each other but say nothing.

The trouble starts right away. Melaku comes back early from the mess hall. Alone. None of us say a word. We know what has happened and there is no point in talking about it. It will only enrage Melaku and it will not bring the boy back. Melaku sits on a pile of rotten cabbage and weeps.

"I only hope that this ends with these tears," Dr. Tesfaye says. "He is such a horribly stupid man." Dr. Tesfaye's eyes are wet and red.

"As long as someone takes care of him," I say, "and they don't pass him around."

"What man would do such a thing? No. Every man will want complete ownership. There will be blood over that boy."

Melaku does nothing stupid and we are relieved. He speaks to no one, but he moves his bedding back over to our side of the room.

36

I do not see the boy for a week, but I have heard what has happened. Somehow everyone but Melaku had missed his arrival at the camp. He was never branded or given a physical. Melaku took him straight to the kitchens. This, however, all changed as soon as Melaku brought him to the enlisted mess hall. The effect was immediate. The boy was taken from Melaku by the first man who saw him come through the door. This guard had the sense to leave with the boy immediately, but the enlisted men live in barracks. There is no place to hide a fourteen-year-old boy. Then there is the rule forbidding prisoners in the barracks. It was Lieutenant

Menna who took him next. He came to investigate the
commotion in the barracks. The men had Adane up on a
table dancing on all fours like a goat. He bleated and but-
ted the soldiers nearest the table. The men cheered each
time he did this. He was wearing nothing but a loincloth
made from the torn material of a red T-shirt. Lieutenant
Menna claimed to be outraged by this behaviour and decided he must take the boy into his custody in order to protect
him. He brought the boy back to his quarters and fed him.
His Fanta was horrified to find the boy in his Lieutenant's
house. This could only mean bad things for the Fanta, so he
told the other Fantas, knowing they would tell everyone
else. They believed him to be exaggerating about the boy's
beauty and charms. Because of this, they made a point to
all come together to witness this supposed wonder. None of
them were disappointed. The Lieutenant's Fanta did his best
to dress Adane up to look like a girl, painting his lips with
red ink and fashioning a makeshift dress from a bed sheet.
The commotion at the Lieutenant's house attracted the
attention of Second Lieutenant Solomon. And so the men
went, like lemmings off a cliff. The Second Lieutenant
brought the boy to his house, much to the relief of
Lieutenant Menna's Fanta. Upon discovering the boy he
stole was stolen, Lieutenant Menna fell into a state beyond
reasoning. He took his pistol and emptied it into the Second
Lieutenant's house. Although no one was hurt, the shooting
attracted the attention of a visiting official from Addis. The
official was outraged. He reprimanded Director Hailu for his
men's repulsive behaviour and went back to Addis to file a
report. Director Hailu confiscated the boy and locked the

men into their houses. We will decide this matter in the morning, one way or the other, he told them and left it at that.

The Fanta Tardesse tells me all of this when I go to collect laundry. I get a similar story at each house, except, of course, at the houses of the two Lieutenants. I duly report all of this to Yonas and Dr. Tesfaye. We decide it is best to keep this information from Melaku.

37

Dr. Tesfaye and I are waiting near the Director's house at dawn. Neither of us say anything. Nothing good is going to happen, so there is really no point in talking about it. Still, we are here. We cannot bear not to know, not to see. Two officers come to the Director's house. They reappear within minutes with the boy and the Director. The four of them walk together to the square in front of the barracks where the men drill daily. We follow, making certain to stay hidden at all times. Dr. Tesfaye is crying, but he is not making a sound. The parade grounds are almost full of guards. I wonder who is guarding the prisoners. It is the most guards I've ever seen in one place at the same time. In the centre of the square there are two parked trucks, and beside them are the two Lieutenants, standing stiffly at attention. The gathering of guards is completely silent. A man coughs. A breeze rustles the grass.

The director walks directly up to the Lieutenants and

immediately slaps each of them across the face. The slaps
echo across the parade grounds like pistol shots. Neither
man moves or changes his expression. The Director makes a
speech. Dr. Tesfaye translates snatches of it, but he is too
caught up in what is happening to do a good job. I understand some of the words myself. Something about
humiliation, the disgrace of the prison, something about
honour. The last words the Director says cause Dr. Tesfaye
to make a choking sound.

He turns to me. "He can't do that," he says.

"What?" I say. "What is he going to do?"

Dr. Tesfaye doesn't answer.

Two officers come forward after the Director finishes
speaking. They attach chains to the boy's arms and legs,
using handcuffs, and then affix the ends of the chains to the
bumpers of two trucks. The Director gives each Lieutenant a
key to a truck. Menna makes a shrieking sound when given
his key and the Director removes his pistol from his holster
and aims it at his head. That's when I leave. I don't walk fast
enough to escape the sound of the engines starting, so I
run, but it is still not quite fast enough. The boy lets out a
single, piercing cry and then there is nothing to hear.

Dr. Tesfaye runs past me, his face wet, his chest hiccup-
ing with sobs.

"Why did you watch?" I yell after him.

He stops running. "I couldn't believe he would actually
make them do it. I thought it was just to scare them."

There's nothing to say, so I say nothing.

"I'm ready to start preparing for your plan," he says.

"I'm prepared. We can leave tonight."

38

The moon follows us across the desert like a hungry dog.
We do not speak. We are too tired and scared. Rocks, thorny
bushes, sand. Sharp dry cold. There is a slight wind. It teases
the loose burlap on our backs and sprays our legs with grit.
We both fall more than once, bruising our knees and ankles.
I had planned to navigate by the stars, which hang like
ornaments, close enough to touch, but I did not take into
account the differences between the North American sky
and the African sky. Nothing is in its proper place. I don't
know why I never noticed this before. We set off in the
direction we know is south and hope we can maintain a
straight line. After an hour we are swallowed up completely
by the bleak waste, and it seems highly probable that we
will not find our way out again. At the first hint of light in
the sky, we dig, taking turns with the shovel. The soil is
rocky. We both have blisters before we excavate two feet of
soil. By the time the sky is pink we are too tired to continue. We cover ourselves with burlap and sand, nestle into our
shallow trench and fall off into sleep as though we jumped
from a cliff.

39

Something is resting on my face. I do not know what it is because there is burlap covering my head, but I know it was not there when I went to sleep. It is much too heavy to be an insect or a mouse. There is only one thing it can be. Sweat has dribbled from my forehead down into my empty eye socket and pooled there. It is the only cool spot on my body. I try to breathe slowly, not to panic. There is just one solution to this problem. I'll do it at the count of three. One. Two. Three. I push up with all the force I am capable of and jump away from the hole. Dr. Tesfaye sits up and screams hoarsely. He wears an expression of utter bewilderment. I don't think he knows where he is. The snake undulates off into the rocks and I sit down and laugh.

40

Once we get moving again, we feel better. We believe we have overcome the most difficult part of the escape. Our stride is long and optimistic. The sun is a smoldering tangerine. We keep it on our left. Dr. Tesfaye suggests a sing-a-long of his favourite American songs. These include

"Country Road," by John Denver, and the theme song from the movie *Titanic*, the name of which escapes both of us.

"Maybe," I suggest after we've exhausted our repertoire of songs, "they'll just assume that the desert swallowed us up and we died."

"I don't think so," Dr. Tesfaye says.

"Why not?"

"Director Hailu is from Gojam. Gojamees will wait an entire lifetime to get revenge. He will lose his honour if he does not get us. It will be better to die in the desert than be caught. He will punish us horribly."

"Yes," I say, thinking of Adane.

"It will be worse than Adane," Dr. Tesfaye says. We have begun to finish each other's thoughts.

"Why?"

"He wasn't punishing Adane. He was punishing the Lieutenants."

"Well, then we can't get caught."

"No."

41

I turn to ask Dr. Tesfaye a question about dehydration and he is gone. He has stopped a hundred yards back and is kneeling down to examine something in the sand.

"What is it?" I say as I walk back.

He holds something up, something yellow, but I can't make it out until I get closer. It is a perfectly ripe banana.

There is not a blemish on it. The skin is moist and the underside is cool. Dr. Tesfaye looks up into the sky.

"Do you think it fell from a plane?" he asks.

"Surely, that would have squashed it."

Dr. Tesfaye peels the banana. As he is passing me half, he stops.

"What?" I say. He looks truly alarmed.

"Of course," he says, "what an idiot I am."

He hands me my half of the banana. I eat it very slowly, chewing each bit carefully and relishing the sweetness. I swallow the last bite and it occurs to me what he is talking about.

"Shit," I say.

"Yes," he says, "they must be close."

We still have several hours of darkness.

"Should we just stop and dig the deepest hole we can? Or move on?"

He says nothing. He walks in a widening spiral around the place where he found the banana. He stops and kneels.

"They are in a Land Rover."

"Are they in front of us or behind us?"

Dr. Tesfaye shakes his head. "I don't know what to do. It seems impossible they did not see us."

I look at my hands. They are cracked and oozing from digging.

"Let's walk," I say.

42

We start to dig the trench later than usual. The sun is above the horizon before we finish. Its heat punishes us. In the distance, I think I see the dust cloud of a moving vehicle. Dr. Tesfaye shades his eyes and squints.

"No," he says, "I don't know."

"It could be the wind."

43

There is only one can of water left. We bury the empty can and decide to drink only three times a day.

44

"How did you lose your eye?" Dr. Tesfaye asks.

The moon is nearly full and we cast long shadows across the sand. There are fewer rocks now, which is good because one of my shoes has fallen apart and my foot is bruised and sore.

"It's a stupid story," I say.

Dr. Tesfaye chuckles. "Of course it is."

He smiles at me when I look at him. His face is drawn and there are scabs on his lips where they have cracked. It looks like smiling hurts him. His legs are two over-ripe bananas, speckled with bruises and scabs. One long scratch runs from his knee to his ankle. It looks sore and ugly. He does not remember where or when he got it.

"When I was five years old," I say, "I was in love with the moon. It was my life's ambition to visit the moon, maybe even live there. I drew pictures of the moon when I was bored in school. There were many posters of the moon on the walls of my bedroom."

Dr. Tesfaye nods his head, watching his feet as he walks. Here, in the desert, it is important to watch out for snakes.

"One day I decided that I could not wait to go to the moon any longer, so I decided to build a tower that would stretch up into the sky, and in that way, I would reach the moon. My neighbourhood was a new one and there were several houses under construction. After school, when the workers had left for the day, I would walk down to the construction sites and get scrap wood. Behind the house in which I lived, there was a small wooded area with a clearing in the centre. I decided this would be the perfect place to build my tower. I borrowed my father's hammer and collected nails at the building sites, each day adding several more boards. When it was nearly as tall as me, I climbed on top of it to test its sturdiness. The test failed and I came tumbling down in a pile of jagged wood and bent nails. One of the nails went right into my eye."

We walk, sand crunching beneath our feet. There is no wind. Dr. Tesfaye continues to look at the ground as we walk. His lips are pressed tight. Finally, he smiles.

"That is a lie, isn't it?" he says.

"Well, that isn't how I lost my eye, but the rest is true. And, I might have been a little younger with the moon part. I did try to build a tower and it fell on me."

"That's what I thought. You don't tell stories that way when you're telling the truth. That is your made-up story voice."

"The real story isn't very nice."

Dr. Tesfaye pats me on the shoulder. He is a very physical man and sometimes likes to hold my hand as we walk. Although it's common for friends to hold hands here, it made me uncomfortable at first, but it no longer does.

I hold my breath and scratch at the patchy beard that has formed over the last half-year or however long it's been since I was swallowed by the world.

"My wife and I—" I stop. The story is simple, but this only makes it more difficult to tell.

"You have a wife. Why would you not tell me such a thing before?"

"She's dead now."

"I see."

"My wife and I were walking from our car to a restaurant. This was in Savannah, a city in the state of Georgia. It was dark. Two men approached us. They both carried baseball bats, thick wooden sticks." I demonstrate their size with my hands. He nods. "They wanted our money. They were nervous and angry. I gave them my wallet, but my wife's purse got snagged on her dress. I don't know what they thought. I think, maybe they thought she was going to run. I don't know. But one of them swung his bat and struck her across the head. A piece of tooth hit me in the eye. Then they ran."

"This is a horrible thing," he says. "I would rather die than watch my wife die."

"She did not die then. They put her in the hospital and she was in a coma for nearly four years."

"Four years? This would not be possible in Ethiopia."

"The doctors told me her brain was dead and I thought it would be best just to let her die, but her parents wouldn't allow it."

"Four years," he says. "I am sorry. I did not think the story would be like that. You sometimes have funny bad luck. I thought the story would be comical."

"That's all right," I say. "I'm glad I told you. I came here to get away from it, but I see now that this is a stupid way to think. Anyway, here, everyone has a story like that."

"Yes," he says, "this is true."

45

Something bites me on the arm while I am sleeping. It feels like my arm has been doused in kerosene and set aflame. There is nothing to do about it but to hurt. And this I do a lot. The pain increases. Dr. Tesfaye examines it and decides it is not a snake bite, but he doesn't know anything beyond that. There are many things that could bite you here, he says.

I cannot sleep because of the pain and so we start to walk early. I tie a piece of burlap above my eyebrows and rub dark dirt beneath my eyes, but there is no way to escape the sun. My face becomes a blister, then a sore.

As soon as the sun sets, we hear the coughing barks of hyenas. The sound unsettles me even though I have heard it before. Their calls to one another sound like the prescient messages of supernatural beasts. I know it is silly and dangerous to ascribe meaning like this. Looking for omens is destructive, but I cannot seem to help it.

"What does that mean?" I ask. "The hyenas? I haven't heard them since we left the camp."

"We must be near other people or water," he says, "but I am only guessing on the top of my head."

This straightforward answer soothes me beyond its meaning. I realize for the hundredth time I could not have done this on my own.

"Don't worry," Dr. Tesfaye says, putting his hand on my shoulder, "they prefer to eat dead people."

46

"My father was a very funny man," Dr. Tesfaye says. "He told me the sky was God's skin."

We are in trouble. I have lost my other shoe, and even though my feet are wrapped in burlap, they are bruised deeply and feel foreign, like lumps of meat. My arm is swollen from the mysterious bite and is nearly twice its normal size. We have run out of food and we are only allowing ourselves three sips of water a day. This morning we agreed to save our urine and drink it. Dr. Tesfaye tells me that since we have been eating almost nothing, the urine will be mainly water anyway. I am surprised at how little this bothers me. Dr. Tesfaye runs a constant fever. He is often confused about where we are and what we're doing. Sometimes he thinks I am his brother Alemu and asks me about his parents. Has his father's knees gotten worse? Do they have enough money? His lips are one big scab. He falls down frequently. Although we do not say it, we both know it.

"One day, I decided to go and touch God's skin. After all, the sky was just over the next hill. I was small. Probably the same age you built your trash pile to the moon. My mother often told me I was not allowed to leave the hill our house was built on, but the sky looked very close. A walk of twenty minutes at the most. So off I went. God's skin was not behind the next hill. It was behind the hill after that. I walked all morning from hill to hill, expecting to touch the sky at each one. By lunchtime, I was lost and hungry. I sat down on a rock and cried. I think I cried because I couldn't climb to the sky, as much as I cried because I was lost. Luckily, a friend of my father's found me on his way home from the market town. When I told him what I was doing, he thought a fever had driven the senses out of my head. I wasn't punished when I got home because my father thought it was so funny. My mother was angry, but my father just laughed and laughed."

"I feel like that now," I say.

"So do I, but I do not think my father's friend is coming."

47

It is dusk. The entire world is the colour of a wilted tea rose. Sky and sand and thorn trees. A ghost moon rises in the east. A ragged nail paring of a moon. We stop to look at it. Dr. Tesfaye says it looks like the blade of a scythe. We each take a shallow sip of warm urine from the can. Our legs no longer belong to us and they will only obey the harshest orders. We are careful not to stop too long for fear of not being able to start again. A pale ribbon of dust appears on the horizon. We stop walking to watch its progress. Its meaning is not apparent at first and then it is.

"There is no reason to run," Dr. Tesfaye says. "It will only make us more tired and then they will catch us anyway."

"I don't think I can run."

"No," he says.

We sit down.

"Perhaps it's someone friendly," I say.

"I don't think so," he says.

"I don't either."

There is nothing else to say. We are too tired.

The dust becomes a truck. An olive green truck with black numbers painted on its side becomes a truck we know. It is indeed trouble and we can only wait for it to reach us. The truck is moving fast, and I think for a moment it is going to run us down, but it slides to a stop several yards in front of

us. The dust behind it blows away and the door opens, but
no one gets out. The windshield is powdered with yellow
dust. It is impossible to see who is inside. Just two dark
shapes coming together and separating behind the glass. The
truck's headlights watch us for several minutes. Finally,
Director Hailu jumps down, followed by another man I do
not recognize. The other man is wearing a guard's uniform
and carrying an AK-47 slung on his shoulder. Director Hailu
has a piece of rusty metal in his hand. Out of habit, we
stand as he approaches. He is talking even before he is close
enough to be heard. During my time in the camp, I learned
some rudimentary Amharic, but he is speaking so quickly I
can only make out the stray word. Water, walking, old man.
If I didn't know who he was, I would think he was glad to
see us. He stops just short of giving us each a hug. He even
pats Dr. Tesfaye on the shoulder.

"What is he saying?"

"He admires our courage."

Hailu says something to Dr. Tesfaye, something cheerful-
sounding but brusque, and Dr. Tesfaye sits down in the
sand. I sit next to him. I wonder how he is going to kill us. I
am exhausted, but my mind is sharpened by adrenaline.
Hailu beckons the soldier over and directs him to hold Dr.
Tesfaye by the arms. The man sets his rifle down in the
sand. Hailu kneels down beside me and hands me the piece
of metal in his hand. It is a pair of old pliers with a sharpened end. He points to Dr. Tesfaye's legs, says something
softly and smiles.

"What is it?" I ask.

"This is where it starts." Dr. Tesfaye closes his eyes.

"What does he want?"

"You must pull out my toenails. It is our punishment for escaping. He says if you pull out the toenails on one of my feet and I pull out the toenails on one of your feet, he will let us live."

"I'm not sure I believe him."

I look at Hailu and he nods at me, smiling. His face seems unnaturally round and it glistens as though rubbed with oil. He points again at Dr. Tesfaye's feet. I shake my head. Hailu says something to Dr. Tesfaye. He no longer pretends to be pleasant.

"He is now saying that if we do not do these things he will get a blowtorch out of the truck and burn us slowly."

Hailu says something. He smiles.

"And, he will make us eat each other bit by bit." Hailu watches me closely as Dr. Tesfaye translates, hoping, no doubt, to see the fear in my face. I am careful to keep my expression neutral. I am almost too tired to be scared, but not quite.

The other soldier says something and laughs.

"The sweat will be our seasoning," Dr. Tesfaye translates.

"I don't want to pull out your toenails," I say.

"It is going to end badly for us no matter what. If he is angry, it will only be worse. Pull them out." He unlaces his shoe and pulls it off slowly. There are three large holes in the sole and his sock comes apart like wet newspaper when he removes it.

"Dr. Tesfaye—"

Hailu pulls a revolver from the holster on his belt and points it at my groin.

"Pull them out," Dr. Tesfaye says again.

"I'm sorry," I say, leaning in towards him. "I'm sorry."

"Pretend you are pulling up a carrot."

I attach the pliers to the toenail on his big toe. It is long and horny and provides an easy grip, but when I yank up, his foot comes with it. It is hard to find the resolve to pull as hard as I must.

Hailu shakes his head and moves over to sit on Dr. Tesfaye's leg, so it will be easier for me to pull the toenails out. With both hands, I pull as hard as I can. Sweat beads up on my forehead and drips down my nose. There is a wet, tearing sound and the nail comes partially free. Dr. Tesfaye screams. It is such a terrible sound it goes right into my nervous system. I pull five or six more times with all the strength I have, hoping that it will hurt him less once it's removed than it does while I'm pulling it out. Each time I pull, Dr. Tesfaye screams that same terrible scream and I feel like a vicious, horrible fuck.

"I'm sorry," I say to Dr. Tesfaye, "I'm sorry." Tears make the sores on my face sting.

"Pull it out." His voice comes from somewhere down below his stomach. It is guttural and ragged with pain.

I pull again. And again. Finally, the toenail comes free with the viscous sound of something being removed from thick mud. A two-inch strip of skin comes off along with it, dangling from the nail like a root. The toenail grows down deep into the flesh of his toe and leaves a gory hole the size of an eye socket once it's gone. Blood runs down his instep and spills onto the sand. Dr. Tesfaye sobs and retches. I toss the toenail away and dry heave several times. There is noth-

ing in my stomach but a tablespoon of urine. I want to wait
a moment before I continue, but Hailu yells and points at
the next toe with the barrel of his gun. He is smiling and his
eyes are glazed over. I attach the pliers to the next nail. Tears
are making it difficult for me to see what I am doing. My
arms ache from the exertion. The second toe requires fifteen
hard pulls to bring it out. Dr. Tesfaye makes choking sounds.
His voice is hoarse. The screams have scraped his vocal
chords raw. The skin on his face is the colour of cigarette
ash. My arms tremble. The guard holding him from behind
says something to Hailu and they laugh. I stop and look at
the guard. A furious energy is rising in me. For the first time
in my life, I feel capable of killing someone. Hailu shouts at
me, spraying my cheek with spittle, and points again to the
foot with his gun. The third toenail is diseased. It crumbles
like stale bread each time I try to get a purchase on it. I
move on to the next one. Blood is dripping from his foot
and soaking into the sand. There is a stain in the sand the
size of a manhole cover. Even as I am disgusted to see it, I
am wishing it were water, which further disgusts me for
thinking such a thing at a time like this. I am utterly
exhausted. I pull at the fourth toe, but I do not have the
strength to get it out. Hailu shouts something at me and the
guard laughs, casually kicking at Dr. Tesfaye's back as he
does so. It is this laugh that sets me off. The anger comes up
from the base of my groin and charges through my limbs like
the spray of electricity made by a live wire dropped into a
puddle. When it reaches my legs, I leap forward and push the
pliers into Hailu's throat. He fumbles the gun and puts his
hands to his throat, gurgling. His eyes are wide with horror

and surprise. The gun falls and bounces off my leg. I pick it up before I even think about it or think about what I've just done and I point it at the guard. I have the clean, bitter taste of murder in my mouth; and in my mind, I'm already ahead of the bullet. I have a clear vision of what will happen to his head when I push the gun against it and pull the trigger and I want it badly and I'm putting pressure on the trigger to make it all come true when Dr. Tesfaye shouts. I stop and look at him. I know that I would have pulled the trigger if Dr. Tesfaye had not shouted stop. The guard releases Dr. Tesfaye and puts his hands up. He is so surprised he just stands and stares. He is shaking now because he can see in my face how much I wanted to end his life. I'm shaking, too, and I still want to do it. It is a desire as simple and powerful as hunger or thirst.

48

Dr. Tesfaye is no longer Dr. Tesfaye. His anger has transformed him. All the muscles in his face are taut and his eyes are darker. While he screams at the soldier in Amharic, he bares his teeth like a cornered dog and flails his arms. He did not stop me from shooting the soldier to save his life. He wants the soldier to suffer the way we have suffered. We will take the truck and leave him here in the sand with Hailu's body.

There is a problem with the keys to the truck. We cannot find them. The guard does not have them, even though he was driving, and they are not in the ignition or anywhere in the cab. They must be in Hailu's pocket or lost somewhere in the sand, but neither of us wants to touch him. Dr. Tesfaye finds a shirt in the back of the truck and goes about bandaging his foot with it. The guard is tied up with his own shirt. I measure my feet against his. They are approximately the same size. I take his boots. They are a little too big, so I pad the toes with pieces torn from his foul smelling socks.

The guard watches me carefully as I kneel down beside Hailu's body. He is watching to see what is in store for him. Going through Hailu's pockets makes me uncomfortable. His eyes are open and blood still oozes out of the wound in his neck. He seems to be looking at me. I keep reminding myself that he was going to kill me. There was no other option. You had no choice. I chant this to myself. You had no choice. Still, there is a pressure building in the back of my head. Here is a dead man. I took his life. This can't be true. This isn't real. Now that I'm no longer in the moment it hardly seems possible I've done this thing. But I can see this is the river which will divide my life. I cannot think about this now. It will do no good. It feels dangerous. I'm afraid of what I'll decide. I'm afraid of what it means. There will be time for guilt when we are safe.

Hailu's right pocket contains a small knife, a box of matches and a crumpled package of cigarettes. I decide to take his clothes, so I unfasten his belt and unzip his pants. Something snags the plastic sack I wear as a shirt and it tears. I reach down to untangle it and—Hailu is not dead. He clenches the plastic sack in his hand and makes a gurgling sound. I slip out of the sack, pulling it over my head and leave it in his hand. He looks at me and I cannot look away. And then, gradually, gradually, his irises lighten and become almost gray. I see it end, his consciousness, like the screen of a television fading out. The gurgling stops and his eyes close. I watch for something to leave his body—I don't know what I'm looking for, a wisp of smoke, a luminous cloud, a crackle of sparks—but nothing happens; he's just dead.

The keys are in the left pocket. My hands shake as I pull off the rest of his clothes. When I put them on, I can smell his living sweat. Again I feel like throwing up, but there is nothing in my stomach. I light one of Hailu's cigarettes with one of his matches. It is stale and wretched tasting.

We untie the guard before we leave. In the rearview mirror, I can see him putting on Hailu's boots as we drive away.

49

I drive. Dr. Tesfaye rummages through the heaps of trash on the floorboards. It no longer seems like the same desert when you are driving in a truck. Dr. Tesfaye makes a yelping sound of joy. He holds up a large canteen. It is full. We both begin to cry.

50

"Will someone be coming after us?" I ask.

"Of course," Dr. Tesfaye says. "He is the director."

"But they may not know where he is. He may be the only one who was looking for us."

"That is true, but there could be more. They could be any-where. They may have passed us; they could be ahead of us."

It is too dangerous to drive on in the dark. The moon is too small to give off much light and there are more and more large, sharp rocks, any one of which could puncture the tires. We park the truck and sleep in the cab. Hyenas bark throughout the night.

51

I teach Dr. Tesfaye how to drive. He is very happy about this. I have always wanted to learn, he says, since I was a boy. Although it hurts his foot, he insists that he can do it. He uses his heel to depress the clutch, which is so loose it requires only the slightest pressure. Even so, he winces each time he uses it. Once the truck is in gear, he only needs his good foot to press the accelerator and it no longer bothers him at all. It takes almost an hour to learn the rudimentary skills, but it is worth it. When the desert becomes smooth again, it means we can take turns and drive straight through without stopping. There is a full barrel of gas in the back and a compass built into the dashboard to guide us. Possibility fills the cab of the truck like sweet smelling incense.

The truck is an old one and it creaks when it is forced to turn sharply. The shocks are worthless and every time we bounce, Dr. Tesfaye groans. I know his foot is causing him enormous pain, but he says nothing about it. He concentrates on the world directly in front of the truck like he is reading a book. He cannot drive fast because of the rocks and his nervousness about being behind the wheel. We creep along. The heat and the motor are hypnotic. I fall asleep.

52

"Ronald, Ronald, wake up. There is a problem."

I jerk awake, twitchy and nervous. It is late afternoon. My eyes are gummy and I have a headache. Smoke pours from the hood of the truck. I hear birds. We are parked beneath an acacia tree. There is grass. I look around, amazed. There is a hopeful, green smudge on the horizon.

"What?" I say, confused. I am staring at the smoke, but it doesn't have meaning. It is white and acrid.

"The truck," he says, opening his door.

The truck is burning. There are flames licking out from beneath the hood.

"How did this happen?" I say. The engine is still running and several danger lights are glowing red. I lean over and turn it off. The gearshift is stuck in first gear. Why didn't I notice that before I fell asleep? This is my fault. "Were you driving this whole time in first gear?"

"Yes," he says, "like you told me."

"And then?"

"The smoke just came out." He pulls my shirt. "Get out before it burns you."

I am still groggy, so it takes a moment to pull myself together and get out of the truck. I pop the hood, releasing the latch and pushing the hot metal up with a stick. I know nothing about engines, but this one looks beyond repair. There appears to be a crack in the engine block, if that is the engine block. It is only smoldering now, but several of the hoses are melted through.

"Can you fix it?" Dr. Tesfaye asks.

"Can you?"

We laugh.

"It was a nice day of driving, Ronald."

"It was."

Dr. Tesfaye sits down to rewrap the bandage on his foot and I go back to the truck to see what we should take from it before it burns. Dr. Tesfaye is convinced it will explode any moment now like a car in a movie. I roll up the shovel in the burlap and put Hailu's pistol in its holster and strap it around my waist. When I check the AK-47, I find there is no ammunition in it, so I leave it. There is still water in the canteen Dr. Tesfaye found and there is another one beneath the seat that is almost full. In the glove compartment, there is a small jar of pills, a pair of canvas gloves and a plastic bag of *quanta*, dried sheep meat. In a blue plastic sack on the floor, there are four over-ripe mangos. I roll all this up in a piece of dry, rotted canvas from the back of the truck and tie it, so it can be slung across my back.

Dr. Tesfaye is still inspecting his foot when I finish. I hand him the jar of pills. He looks at them carefully and shrugs.

"Nothing," he says, tossing them away.

"Oh, well," I say.

"I have some bad news," he says.

"What is it?"

"My toes are infected."

I kneel down and look at them. They are swollen and angry looking. Pus is oozing from the big toe.

"Can you walk?"

"I must."

Before we leave, I break a branch from the acacia tree and cut the thorns off with Hailu's knife. I give this to Dr. Tesfaye to use as a walking stick and I shoulder up my bundle. We start off again toward the smudge of green on the horizon. Dr. Tesfaye walks very slowly and with great pain. He winces with each step. The truck is still smoking when we leave. For an hour or so, every time I turn around, I can see our possibilities drifting up into the empty blue sky.

53

We stop and rest once an hour, and even at this slow pace, I notice the landscape is changing. We are no longer in the desert. Twice we see herds of cows, but no one is watching them. Dr. Tesfaye believes that the boys herding them hide when they see us coming.

"It is not often that a white man comes to this part of the country, much less one who looks as strange as you," he says.

"What do you mean?" I say. "I'm wearing normal clothes now."

We are sitting on a rock beneath an acacia tree. The land slopes down before us. Big pillow stuffing clouds move across the horizon, creating shadows on the grassy hills below. The shadows look like purple pools of water.

"Your hair looks like a fiery bush." He coughs when he laughs and grimaces with pain.

I touch my head. The hair is knotted and burred. The clumps of hair are not even dredlocks, just a matted mess. I haven't seen my own reflection since the day I found the child's body.

"They probably think you are a demon," he says, smiling.

54

We stop an hour after sunset because Dr. Tesfaye can no longer go on. His face is ashy from the pain. We sleep in the tall grass beneath an acacia tree. There is a slight breeze and it makes the branches click. I dream of drinking beer. It is cold and delicious and comes in mugs the size of my head. No matter how much I drink I don't get drunk. We wake up cold and shivering and damp with dew. When Dr. Tesfaye unwraps his foot, some of the skin comes off. Dark lines stretch up his foot. It smells like rotten chicken.

"Blood poisoning," he says. "It probably came from those rusty pliers."

"What does that mean?"

"I need antibiotics."

55

By early afternoon, Dr. Tesfaye cannot walk another step. The landscape has changed from yellow and beige to pale green. The hills are spotted with huge fig trees and the occasional stand of eucalyptus. We settle down to rest on a small rise above a syrup-slow trickle of a stream. Its water is the colour of strong coffee and the banks are mashed with hundreds of hoof prints. The grass is green and soft here, though cropped nearly to the roots. It gives the countryside the look of a manicured park. On the other side of the stream, there is a grove of banana trees, but they have no fruit. We sit without speaking. Pain has carved deep creases in Dr. Tesfaye's cheeks. He lies back and stares at the sky for hours. He does not even move his eyes. I have many things I would like to discuss with him—Hailu, our pursuers, the condition of his foot, our options, but I do not want to bother him while he is so tired. There are only two things we can do now. I can go and look for help or we can stay together and wait.

In the early evening, Dr. Tesfaye rouses and we make a meal of quanta and warm water and a mango. It is a feast and it makes me optimistic. Just before the sun goes down, we spot a dust cloud behind us. It is far away, somewhere at the edge of the desert, and it could just as easily be a gust of wind as it could a truck. I had planned on lighting a fire, but this no longer seems like a good idea. Somewhere in the small valley below us there is a large herd of cows. We hear them lowing all evening, but we cannot see them.

Once it is dark, the singing starts. The song is sung through call and return. A single person, a young boy maybe, sings a measure in a high plaintive voice and then a group of twenty or so men sing it back to him. The singing is accompanied by the clomping sound of hooves. It gets closer and closer. The singing is both beautiful and terrible. Even if we could have, I don't think we would have moved.

The first horseman stops when he sees us. It is dark, but I can see he holds a long spear with a tip the size of a bayonet and is dressed in a red and black tunic. He turns his horse and disappears. Within moments there are at least twenty riders surrounding us. One man climbs down from his horse and approaches us. He has an AK-47 and a spear. He stares at us for a while before speaking, his eyes making slow paths from our faces to our feet and back again. When he finishes speaking, Dr. Tesfaye responds. The man looks behind him and another man steps down from his horse. He is tall and carries two AK-47s, one on each shoulder. He speaks to Dr. Tesfaye. Inexplicably, Dr. Tesfaye laughs. So does the tall man. They talk for several minutes before he turns to me and translates.

"These are Gudji warriors."

"Do they want our cocks?"

"No," he smiles uncomfortably. "I don't think so."

"What do they want?"

"They want to trade."

The Gudji make no sound, but the horses nicker and snort and stomp. Their eyes are bright in the darkness. Each man watches us with an expression of alert indifference. They look neither hostile nor friendly.

"We don't have anything to trade."

"They want your gun."

"This doesn't sound like trading."

"It's not. It's more like honourable theft. This way we don't lose respect."

"That's polite," I say. "What will they give us in return?"

"I don't know."

"If it is a trade, then they must give us something in return." I know I should be frightened, but I am far too tired. These men can take nothing from me but my life.

Dr. Tesfaye turns and talks to the tall Gudji again. I have an idea. I touch Dr. Tesfaye on the shoulder.

"Ask him if they will give us a horse or two."

Dr. Tesfaye asks and the warrior laughs.

"I take that as a no."

"A gun is too small to trade for a horse."

"Maybe just a ride to Kenya. They're going in the right direction."

This time the man nods as Dr. Tesfaye speaks, then he turns to the man beside him and they confer.

"Do you know their language?" I ask him.

"No," Dr. Tesfaye says, "but the tall one knows some Amharic."

Dr. Tesfaye and the warrior talk again and this time they both laugh.

"Do we have anything else we can trade?"

"I don't think so," I say. "We need everything else."

Dr. Tesfaye looks through the bundle of our things. There is nothing, really. It's just trash.

"Wait," I say and I remove my glass eye.

The men make a sighing sound. In the dark, it must look like I am plucking out my living eye. I hand it over to Dr. Tesfaye, who in turn gives it to the warrior translator. He takes it with great care and holds it in the bowl of two cupped hands. The men on horses lean over to get a better look. Only now do they seem like humans and not some sort of ghost warriors.

"Tell him it will give him powerful visions if he holds it when he sleeps."

Dr. Tesfaye explains. The warriors discuss this among

themselves for some time, passing around my eye and exclaiming over it. Finally, the translator speaks again.

"They have agreed to take us as far as the black road in Kenya," Dr. Tesfaye says.

"The black road? That sounds like the highway from Addis. From there we could catch a ride."

The horses are small, ponies almost, and prone to snapping at you with their long, yellow teeth. At the rear of the party, there are several unmanned horses, which aren't being used to carry packs. These are the ones we will ride. Dr. Tesfaye has never ridden a horse and is extremely nervous, but once he gets into the saddle he is fine.

"Just don't fall off," I tell him.

The last time I rode a horse was at a pony ride at the Bulloch county fair. I think I was six. The horse was piebald and morose and punished its riders with bouts of foul-smelling flatulence. I may be wrong, but I seem to remember its name was Winifred.

56

We ride through the night with twenty warriors, three young boys and a herd of emaciated cattle. Fifty or sixty bony steers with horns two feet in span. In the dark, the landscape means nothing. We are going up or we are going down. The men sing the entire time. I nod off and jerk awake. Dr. Tesfaye sleeps with his body bent in half, his head almost resting on the horse's neck. We stop at sunrise

to water the horses and eat. The Gudji share their meal with
us, which consists of some sort of bean mush and a smoky-
tasting drink. After the initial conversation, they do not
speak. Not even amongst themselves. The hills roll beneath
us, lush and green. We ford shallow streams lined with
banana and jacaronda trees. Sometimes in the distance,
there are villages, but we avoid them. Tiny settlements of
five or six round mud houses thatched with banana leaves
and ringed by kitchen gardens. From each roof comes a
bluish haze of smoke. Once we surprise two boys playing a
game with pebbles on a flat, gray table of rock. They scam-
per off into the undergrowth like startled rabbits. The men
laugh. When the sun sets, the party stops to rest in a grove
of acacia trees. Some of the men dismount and sleep on the
packed clay, the rest remain on their mounts. Within three
hours, we are in the saddle again, moving through grass
high enough to brush against my hanging feet. The meat of
my ass is sore and my inner thighs are chafed.

The sun rises on a different landscape. Steep forested hills
and dramatic gorges. Streams of clear water with rocky bot-
toms. We stop again to drink and eat. Dr. Tesfaye unwraps his
foot. The smell is startling. The flesh where the nails once were
is now a greenish gray and dark blood poisoning lines go up
his ankle and disappear into his pants.

"That doesn't look good," I say.

"It doesn't hurt as much now."

"Is it gangrenous?"

"Yes. I will lose my toes, maybe my foot." His voice is flat
and hoarse. The whites of his eyes look yellow.

When we climb back into our saddles, Dr. Tesfaye

requires the help of two men. This time there are only five of us. The others remain behind. We ride. Up a slight slope, through trees, and down across another stream and onto a flat plain dotted with acacia trees. After an hour, the horses come to a stop. The tall warrior and the translator ride back and sidle up next to Dr. Tesfaye. They speak for several moments. The warrior points.

"The highway is over there," Dr. Tesfaye explains. "He says it isn't far. They cannot ride into the open. This is not their land. It could mean a fight."

57

The two men wheel their horses around and the group rides off. The tall warrior holds my eye in his hand and waves it at me as he goes. Dr. Tesfaye sits on the ground. His head hangs down onto his chest.

"I can't do it," he says. His voice is far away.

"Yes, you can," I say, "we're almost there."

"I cannot."

I sit down next to him.

"Why don't we rest for a bit? You'll feel better after a while. We've been riding for twenty-four hours."

"It's not just that."

"Let's just rest and then we'll see." I say this, but I'm not sure I believe it will make a difference.

We lie in the grass. I close my eyes and sleep immediately.

58

When I awake, Dr. Tesfaye is already sitting up. His foot is unwrapped. It no longer looks much like a foot, more like the corpse of a small creature attached to the bottom of his leg. The skin has split in several places and the flesh beneath is the colour of fresh tuna. Flies cover the toes.

"Should you do that? Won't they lay eggs?"

"That's what I'm hoping."

"Jesus, why?"

"The maggots will eat the diseased flesh. It could save me if nothing else does."

"Won't they eat the healthy flesh, too?"

"I don't think so."

"Can you walk on it?"

"No. I think you should go ahead, and if you find someone, bring them back to get me."

"I don't know."

"It's the only way."

"Maybe we could make a crutch from a tree branch and—"

"No." He smiles. "It's useless. As long as I am still, it is fine. See?" He flicks his toes with a finger. They make a wet pop. The flies rise and whine and then resettle to eat and lay eggs. "I feel nothing. It is only when I try to walk that it hurts." He smiles again, and in this second smile I see something that disturbs me. It isn't really a smile.

I leave him with the canteen and the shovel and the rest of our gear. I half-drag half-carry him over to the shade of a large acacia tree. I break the thorns off a section of the trunk, each one as sharp and hard as a carpet nail, so he can lean back against it and rest. The muscles in his face are bunched up with pain, but he is smiling. I reach down to shake his hand and he pulls me into an embrace.

"You will find someone and we will be safe," he says.

"I will." I am still unsure about leaving him.

"Hurry," he says.

59

It takes three hours to reach the highway, but it is easy walking. The ground slopes gently, imperceptibly, and there are no vines to catch my feet or rocks to stumble over, only grass. The highway itself is unimpressive. An anticlimax of the most depressing sort. It is barely two lanes and riddled with potholes. The edges have cracked into pieces. I wonder for a time if it is even a highway.

There is nothing to do but wait, so I sit beside the road and construct a chessboard with pebbles and play three games against myself. I am muddled and lose track of which rocks are supposed to represent which chess pieces. Most of the time I just sit and stare. By late afternoon, I hear the rumble of big trucks. There are six of them heading south. The logo of a Japanese car manufacturer and the words 'Kenya-Japan Highway Partnership,' are painted in red on the doors of the cabs, but the trucks themselves are Mercedes. As they approach, I stand and wave my arms above my head. The first truck pulls to the side and stops. The others idle in the road. Inside the cab of the first truck, there is an African and a Japanese man. The two men talk for a moment before they get out and approach me. They are both wearing white jumpsuits with red stripes on the arms and legs. They are puzzled by my appearance. I can see them trying to decide whether or not I am dangerous.

"Do you speak English?" I say.

"Yes," they say in ragged unison.

They stop about ten feet away from me and wait for me to speak. The Japanese man is wearing a baseball cap with the car company's corporate logo embroidered on it. He frets with the bill of the hat and shifts his weight from foot to foot. The African man is tall and thin. He has a neat moustache and a piece of plaid flannel wrapped around his head like a turban. He examines me closely without moving.

"My friend is hurt. He has damaged his foot and cannot walk. I can't carry him to the road. He is just over there."

"I am sorry," the Japanese man says. His voice is neutral. I can't tell whether he means he is sorry my friend is hurt or that he is sorry, but he can't help me. This situation could tilt either way.

"Can you drive over and pick him up? He is just over the rise. I think he may be dying." I don't actually believe this, but it could become true if he doesn't get to a clinic sometime soon.

They walk back to the cab and talk. They talk for almost ten minutes, which doesn't bode well. I kick the rocks off

my makeshift chessboard and clench my hands. The
Japanese man gets out of the truck and speaks with the
man in the truck behind them. I am starting to doubt. I'm
not sure I would be willing to do such a thing if I were in
their position. It sounds like the set-up for an ambush. This
area is famous for its bandits. He returns to his truck and
speaks with the African again. When the door opens once
more, the African man is frowning.

"I am sorry," the Japanese man says.

"Why?" I say. My voice is rising in pitch and sounds
pathetic even to me.

"We cannot take the trucks off the road. It is not permitted.
These trucks are full of materials. They may get stuck."

"But it is just up there. You can almost see him from here."

The African man shades his eyes and looks in the direction
that I have pointed. We do not speak. A breeze rises and stirs
the dust along the shoulder of the road. I can feel the beat of
my heart in my clenched fists.

"I do not see him," the African man says.

"If you can't take the trucks, maybe you could help me carry
him down to the road. He is dying. Please. What do you want
me to do? I'll do it . . . if it's money, as soon as we get to—"

"We do not want money." The African glares at me.

"We must move on," the Japanese man says. "We cannot
stop. I am sorry." He shakes his head, but he will not look me
in the eye. "There are bandits here."

"Can you at least give me a ride to the next town? You
don't seem to understand—" My voice breaks and I am furious.
I am angry with myself. I am angry with these people who
don't seem to care. My head is pounding and my throat is raw.

The Japanese man holds up a finger and then they close the door to the truck and talk amongst themselves. The African man looks upset. He moves his hands around and jerks his head back and forth as he speaks. Their conversation lasts five minutes. Finally, the African opens the door.

"Get into the truck," he says. There is a pistol on the seat between them and the African touches it lightly with his left hand.

I am so tired and relieved I cry. I don't realize I'm doing it until a drop falls from my cheek. The two of them exchange a look when they notice this. They say nothing; however, the tension between us decreases. We do not speak. The truck rumbles to life and the convoy starts out again. The African man turns on the tape deck. It is a wild dance song with many drums. I am blind to the world outside the truck. I slump down in the seat and cover my face with my hands. The African taps the steering wheel in rhythm to the song. The Japanese man crosses and uncrosses his legs.

"What are you doing here?" the Japanese man says.

"I came to work on an irrigation project. Someone tried to kill us." Even these few words require a great deal of effort. The truth is I don't know the answer to that question any longer. It doesn't mean anything, but it is a question everyone asks.

"Who? Who tried to do this thing?"

"A crazy policeman."

The two of them exchange a look that I cannot identify.

I slip into sleep without realizing it. One moment I am staring at the tendrils of raised dust on the floorboards of the truck, my teeth rattling as we roll over potholes and gravel, and the next, the Japanese man is shaking my shoulder.

"What is it?" I say. "Are we in town?"

"They want to see your papers."

We have stopped at a military checkpoint. A cinder block shack. A rusting hulk of a pick-up truck. A chain across the road. Four men with machine guns. There is a fifth man looking in at me through the window of the truck. His face is powdered with orange dust. I can see the reflection of my head in his sunglasses. My cheeks are hollow and my empty socket is inflamed. My hair is matted with dirt and bits of grass. My mouth looks like a shotgun wound. The soldier barks out something I can't understand.

"He says you must get out of the truck," the African man says.

The door is opened and I clamber out. The sun is a malign force. My eye stings and I shade it with my hand. The soldier grabs me by the elbow and pulls me over to the cinder block shack. The African man follows us.

"Show him your papers. Your passport," he says. His voice is sympathetic now.

"They are lost. I don't have them."

The African looks at me with real pity. "This will cause a problem." He turns to the soldier and speaks in a low, soft voice. The soldier turns to me and shouts, poking me in the ribs with the barrel of his gun. The other soldiers laugh. One of them comes over and stands beside me, while the first man goes into the shack. He picks up a phone and speaks. I look at the African man.

"What is happening?"

"They are calling the main station. You will have to stay here until they decide what to do."

"How long will it take?"

The African just looks at me. There is nothing to say to this and I know it.

"Where am I?"

The African tilts his head and frowns.

"This is Kenya, right?" I say. "We are in Kenya?"

"No," the African man says. "That is Kenya." He points down the road. In the distance, there is a collection of buildings. They shimmer in the heat. Somewhere in the bushes nearby there is a goat bleating, but I can't see it. The bell around its neck jangles. It bleats again. The sound is piteous. For a moment I forget about everything but the sound of the goat. Each bleat is higher in pitch.

"Can you tell them about my friend? I can't leave him out there to die by himself."

"I have told him."

"What did he say?"

The man shrugs. "He didn't say anything. It is impossible to talk to men like this. They ask you questions and you give them answers. That is all."

I grind my teeth and stare up into the sky above Ethiopia, above Africa. The sky is so big it obliterates every-thing. It is swallowing me up. I'm drowning in it.

"I must leave now," the African says. "There is nothing more I can do. I am a Kenyan. This will not help you. You need an Ethiopian. Do you know someone?"

I cannot answer because I'm drowning in the sky.

The African grasps my shoulder with his large hand. He gives me an intent look, gently squeezing my shoulder until I nod. Then he turns and walks back to the truck. The first soldier motions to me and yells something. The soldier holding my arm pushes me toward the entrance of the shack. Inside, it is darker. I am blind for a moment. The phone is pressed up against my ear. A man talks to me. His voice is distorted by static on the line. He must repeat himself several times before I understand.

"What is your purpose in Ethiopia?" he asks.

"I am a worker for an international aid organization. I came to work on an irrigation project."

The goat bleats again somewhere out in the bushes behind the guard shack. I raise my head to look. It has become important to me in some vague but pressing way that I get a look at the goat. The sound is closer now, but I still cannot see it. Someone fires off a three-round burst. This is followed by wild laughter. The man on the phone talks and talks, but I can no longer understand him.

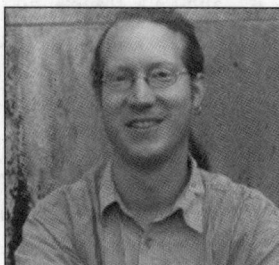

DAVID ZIMMERMAN grew up in Atlanta, Georgia
and later studied film at Emerson College in
Boston. He studied Creative Writing for three
years in Tuscaloosa, Alabama before heading for
the bright lights of New York City, where he
worked as a publicist for St. Martin's Press. He
now divides his time between teaching abroad
(Brazil and Ethiopia) and living and working in
Savannah, Georgia. A later draft of an earlier
3-Day Novel submission won Mr. Zimmerman
the 2001 *Quarterly West* novella contest.